Hear My Love An Anthology of Christian Romance

Michelle David

Published by Trellis Publishing, 2021.

This is a work of fiction. Similarities to real people, places, or events are entirely coincidental.

HEAR MY LOVE AN ANTHOLOGY OF CHRISTIAN ROMANCE

First edition. June 25, 2021.

Copyright © 2021 Michelle David.

ISBN: 979-8224716333

Written by Michelle David.

HEAR MY LOVE

MICHELLE DAVID

Chapter 1

Violet reached for the knob on her stereo and turned the volume all the way up. If she listened very closely through the cloud of silence in her head, she could hear the low thrumming of the cello. The violins were gone. She should be hearing harp, too. Most people who lost their hearing lost the high notes first, and it was no different for her. All she could hear of the London Philharmonic Orchestra was bass and buzzing where once there was Handel's *Rejoicing*.

Angry tears stung her eyes, but she blinked them away. Nancy would be here any minute. Violet didn't want to be crying over her MP3 player when her friend got here.

Even as she thought Nancy's name, a hand landed on her shoulder. Violet yelped and turned, heart thumping. Vertigo gripped her, spinning through her head and swooping through her stomach. She might have fallen if not for the hand that caught her elbow. When her gaze finally steadied, it was Nancy's warm brown eyes and soft face that she saw.

Sorry, Nancy mouthed. Violet's best friend always kept her sentences short these days. She pulled a pained face, and added, *Too loud.*

Violet nodded apologetically and turned back, slowly this time, to click off the stereo. "I'm sorry," she said, and wondered how loud her voice must sound to Nancy if she could hear it herself. Just to be safe, she lowered her volume. "You know how people always ask each other what piece of music they'd choose if they could only hear one more? That was mine."

Nancy's mouth turned down, pitying. *Not the last*, she mouthed. *Have faith.* She pointed upward.

Violet nodded, but she didn't answer. She didn't have much to say to God lately. Ever since she was a child, she'd always believed He was the Great Physician, that He could heal anything if He wanted to. But He had not restored her hearing, no matter how hard she'd prayed.

How could He allow this to happen when He knew how much music meant to her? He had healed millions of people over the course of human existence, but He would not heal Violet.

Nancy reached for Violet's elbow again, and Violet allowed herself to be led forward through her living room. Her head swooped and spun with every step, and her stomach threatened to spill its contents all over her brightly-colored rug and shiny baby grand. She swallowed hard. *Not again,* she thought. Her nausea gradually faded as Nancy led her through her front door.

It was a sunny spring day, with a gem-blue sky overhead and a slight breeze to cool Violet's hot face. The cherry tree in her front yard had, in the last few days since she had dared to venture outside, burst into vibrant flower. Nancy's freshly washed car shone from the driveway where she'd parked. It was a beautiful day. Only Violet's mood was ugly.

Nancy opened the passenger-side door to her car and helped Violet inside.

"And they said chivalry was dead." Violet grinned.

Nancy smiled back, and the edges of her eyes crinkled. *Watch your feet,* she mouthed, shutting the door.

On the way to the hospital, Violet turned her attention to the yards and gardens of the houses they passed. All the grass had turned emerald green, and flowers bloomed riotously from gardens and cracks in sidewalks. *Spring,* she thought, and tried to bring Vivaldi to her mind. The strains of the piece still came easily to her memory, but she'd once been told auditory memories were among the soonest to fade. How long would she have this silent music to draw on for strength in hard times?

Someday, maybe she wouldn't remember what music sounded like at all.

Dr. Minelli's office was on the fourth floor of the hospital, so Nancy helped Violet onto the elevator and steadied her when the upward lurch made Violet fall against the mirrored wall.

Somehow, they made it into the audiologist's waiting room and checked in despite the return of Violet's nausea. It was a restful sort of room, with light blue walls and potted ferns on the tables beside the outdated magazines. A huge aquarium covered one wall, and Violet watched the fish dart back and forth between the glass walls of their home.

Nancy touched her shoulder when the nurse called for her, and together they followed the scrub-wearing man down the hall to a room with drawings of the inner ear on all the walls. Violet sat up on the paper-covered table and Nancy sat in a plastic chair against a wall.

Dr. Minelli wasn't Violet's normal doctor, but they'd met a few times when the pretty, dark-haired audiologist had consulted with old Dr. Farnam. Meniere's disease wasn't uncommon, but it wasn't something Violet's primary had spent a lot of time with, either. Nobody knew what caused the disease. Researchers blamed everything from allergies to autoimmune disorders.

Whatever caused it, the fact remained that Violet had a severe case. Slight vertigo and tinnitus had, over the course of years, degenerated to 90% deafness and vertigo so severe Violet had almost become an invalid. They had tried drugs to reduce fluid in her body, as well as drugs to keep her from becoming too stressed out; they'd given her pills for nausea and more months of physical therapy than she could even count anymore. But none of it had worked. At only twenty-seven years old, Violet was barely able to care for herself. She couldn't drive. She couldn't stand for any length of time. She couldn't even walk down a hallway without supporting herself against a wall.

Medically, they'd come to the last resort. If Violet wanted any hope of a normal life, if she wanted to be able to run in the park again or walk any potential children in a stroller, she had to have this surgery. Not that she'd have much chance for marriage and children without the ability to hear. What husband would have her now? Brian certainly wouldn't be interested in a woman who couldn't even hear him.

When Dr. Minelli finally came into the room, she gave Violet a huge smile and spoke to her in slow, clearly enunciated words. Violet couldn't hear conversational voice levels anymore, but she carefully watched the doctor's lips for information: *remove the labyrinth*, she managed to catch, though it was followed by gibberish. *Permanent deafness. Thursday the twenty-first.*

When Violet finally started to cry, Dr. Minelli's pretty face turned pitying and she placed a hand on Violet's shoulder. *We wouldn't do this unless it was absolutely necessary*, the doctor mouthed. *I'm so sorry.*

"What am I going to do?" Violet sobbed. "I'm a musician! How am I going to live? How am I going to communicate? I can hardly even read lips!"

Dr. Minelli sighed, and though Violet couldn't hear a noise as soft as a breath anymore, she saw the doctor's shoulders heave. She stood up and walked to the sparkling clean counter beside the sink where she'd washed her hands and brought back a pamphlet made of a folded computer print-out. She handed it to Violet, who grasped it as if taking a life preserver.

American Sign Language Classes, it said. A group of smiling people adorned the front cover. If any of them were deaf, Violet couldn't figure out why they looked so happy.

*

Nancy helped Violet into the car and walked around to the driver's side. The day was still beautiful, though the sun had risen enough to heat the inside of the car. Nancy turned on the air conditioner, and it struggled against the late spring weather to keep them cool. Violet watched the scenery roll by until they turned down a road leading away from her house. She shot Nancy a confused look.

"Hey, sis, my house is that way." Violet pointed in the other direction.

Nancy glanced at her passenger. Maybe Violet imagined the sly, slightly guilty look on her face. Then she looked back at the road and said something Violet couldn't translate.

"You have to look at me when you talk or I can't understand you, Nance," Violet said.

They rolled up to a stop sign. Nancy turned her face toward Violet and mouthed, *Going to church. Left my purse.*

Violet groaned. "I'll sit in the car, if that's okay with you. I really don't want a ton of well- meaning people falling over themselves to try to talk to me."

Nancy shook her head. *Pastor wants to see you about insurance*, she said. *You better come in.*

Heavy dread settled in Violet's belly. She couldn't possibly face the pastor, not today. He'd been text-messaging her for the better part of a month, ever since she found out she was going to have to have the labyrinthectomy. He'd been hoping she could return to work on the worship team soon. She'd been ignoring him because she didn't have the heart to tell him she never would. Nancy had told him, of course. It hadn't stopped his texted thoughtfulness.

She couldn't really afford to have her insurance cancelled now, though. The time for ignoring her boss was over.

They pulled into the church's familiar parking lot. Violet waited for her friend to come around and help her out of the car. Even if she was able to stand on her own, she might have stayed where she was until Nancy dragged her out.

The pastor wasn't the only one who'd been texting her. Brian had, as well. If God was listening to her, she'd pray for Brian to be anywhere but here. Of course, God wasn't listening. Not to her. Not today.

She knew he was present as soon as she walked through the church door. She could feel the pulsing of bass guitar through the soles of her flats, which meant he was here, practicing with the rest of the worship team. Practicing without her. Violet trained her eyes on the floor and let Nancy lead her past the nave and down the hall to the pastor's office. She willed Brian not to notice her and not to come out. She thought she'd made it home free when someone touched her elbow.

She looked up into a pair of jade-green eyes. Her heart sped up even as she willed it not to. Brian was as handsome as ever, with his straight, white smile and blond hair brushing his collar. He wasn't wearing his leather motorcycle jacket, which meant he'd draped it over the back of a chair somewhere. Violet made an attempt to return his happy smile, but she knew her own expression was tired and wan.

Hey, he mouthed, and then something garbled. She remembered the sound of his voice, raised in harmony with her own in praise to Almighty God. Now she couldn't even understand what he was saying. Violet frowned, and Brian's face fell. She immediately missed that smile. He lit her up with it. But telling him that would make sure he never left her alone.

"I can't understand you," she said instead. It was true in so many ways. Why did he keep trying to talk to her when he knew she couldn't hear him anymore? Why did he keep trying to convince her to go out with him when she'd made it so very clear that she couldn't?

Brian took a deep breath as if gathering himself. Slowly, carefully, he mouthed, *Did you get my texts?*

She sighed. And what was she supposed to say to that direct a question? Of course she'd gotten them. Her phone worked fine. It was her ears that were messed up.

"I've been busy," she said. "I'm having surgery later this month."

Brian's eyes turned sad, and he reached out to touch her arm again. *I'm so sorry.*

Was that the theme for today? Everybody was so very, very sorry. But none of them had to choose between the ability to walk and the ability to hear. Violet bit her tongue and didn't say that out loud. It wasn't Brian's fault she had this disease.

A finger tapped her arm, and she looked back at Nancy. Nancy gave Brian a twinkling smile. Violet was about to ask what that particular expression was supposed to mean when Nancy mouthed, *Go sit down. I'll bring pastor to you.*

Brian gave Nancy a grateful smile and offered Violet his arm. Oh, *that's* what they were up to. Nancy was trying to play matchmaker again. Violet scowled at her friend and pointedly did not reach for Brian.

"I can walk, thank you," Violet snapped. "I don't need to sit down."

Oh, come on. Brian made a broad gesture with his hands, echoing his mouthed words. *Take a load off.* He smiled again, this time even more charming than before. Nancy gave Violet a little shove, and she suddenly found that she had to take Brian's arm or rely on her own dizzy feet.

He smelled so nice. He always did. She turned to scowl at Nancy, who only smiled and waved. The traitor.

Brian led her to the nave and down to the front row. Her former bandmates stood on the stage behind the pulpit, dressed in casual clothes instead of their Sunday finery. Lisa, the lead singer, grinned and waved as Brian helped Violet take a seat. Randy, lead guitar, set down his instrument and jogged down the stairs. He leaned down gingerly to wrap Violet in a hug. His beard tickled her cheek, but his smile was bright and welcome.

Hey, girl, he mouthed. *Come to watch the auditions?*

"What auditions?" Violet looked up at Brian, who was scowling at Randy. Randy's smile became a chagrined grimace almost instantly and he said something to Brian that Violet couldn't catch.

Brian sighed and Randy moved aside. Brian crouched in front of her chair and mouthed, *Don't freak out.*

"Freak out?" Her stomach felt as if it had suddenly filled with lead and was about to tip over. "Why would I freak out? What's he talking about, auditions?" It clicked all at once. "Oh. I see. You're auditioning a new keyboard player."

Regret turned Brian's mouth down, and she knew she'd guessed correctly. They were filling her old job. They'd been down a keyboard player ever since Violet had been out of work. Of course they needed to fill her spot.

It all made sense to her logical mind. So why did she suddenly want to cry?

She pushed up out of her chair, trying to ignore the spinning in her head. Brian reached out to steady her, but she shrugged his hand away.

"I probably should get out of your way so you can work. I'm sure none of the keyboard players want to audition with your old bandmate watching." She gave Lisa a wave and smiled shakily at Randy. Randy smiled back, but he looked kind of sick and green.

Just once, Lord, she thought. *Just once, let me walk out of here with my dignity intact.* She took a careful step past Brian and pretended she didn't see him reaching protectively after her. Another step, and she was still on her feet. Could she dare to hope that God was actually listening to her for once?

Her head started to spin four steps in. She told herself to ignore it, but after another step she had to steady herself against a pew. She took another step.

It felt like something huge, maybe a giant, was pressing down on the top of her head. Despair flooded her in the split second before she crashed onto the ground.

Violet managed to get her hands between her face and the floor, so she only scraped her palms and bruised her pride. Hot tears stung her eyes. For a long moment, all she could do was kneel on the ground with her head spinning and try not to cry and vomit simultaneously.

It was probably thirty seconds before strong arms lifted her up and held her steady. She found herself pressed against Brian's hard chest and so ashamed she couldn't stand to look into his eyes. He tried to catch her gaze by moving into her line of sight, but Violet looked stubbornly away.

Another set of hands gripped her arm, and she turned to find Nancy beside her, looking regretful and anxious. Violet let her friend lead her away. Her cheeks still burned with shame as Nancy helped her into the car.

They didn't speak at all until they got to Violet's house. Violet wanted to fling open the door and storm inside, but she didn't want to end up sprawled out in her driveway with her neighbors gawking. So she waited for Nancy to come around and help her, even though Nancy was the last person on Earth she wanted to interact with.

Nancy's broad, dark face was mournful. *I'm so sorry,* she mouthed. Violet only scowled. Nancy didn't speak again until Violet was safely ensconced in the floral print easy chair that sat across from her couch.

"Why did you take me in there?" Violet demanded. "I didn't even get a chance to see the pastor! Did he really ask to see me?"

Nancy flushed so deeply that Violet knew he hadn't. *Brian asked to see you,* she mouthed. *He said he misses you.*

"He *misses* me! Nancy, I've told you a hundred times that I can't focus on dating right now. I can't understand a word he says. How am I supposed to carry on a relationship with a man I can't even hear?"

Nancy's jawline firmed up, and her dark eyes flashed. *You say that about everything. 'How am I supposed to do anything when I can't even hear?' You've stopped living. I never thought you were the type to roll over and die, but I guess I was wrong.*

Violet was so stunned she couldn't reply.

Brian cares about you, Nancy continued. *He always has. He doesn't care if you're deaf, or if you can play the piano anymore. He cares about you as a person.* She paused, and her angry face softened. *You're the only one who cares about that stuff, Vi. The rest of us just want you to be happy again. There was a time when Brian made you happy.*

"Do you know what made me happy?" Violet demanded. "Making music with the worship team made me happy. But I can't do that anymore, can I? And thanks to you, I am fully aware that they're replacing me!"

Nancy's eyes narrowed. Violet let her gaze follow Nancy all the way to the door as she waited for a response, but instead Nancy left the room and slammed the door behind her.

*

Around the house, when she was alone, Violet used a walker to get from place to place. She didn't always need it, but it kept her from falling down when the vertigo hit. It reminded her of when her grandmother used to toddle around her nursing home. Violet couldn't bring herself to add tennis balls to the feet. Just using the walker made her feel a hundred years old.

She decided on a salad for dinner, and shuffled around her kitchen with her walker, thinking more about what Nancy had said to her than about the tomatoes she was trying to cut. *I never thought you were the type to roll over and die.* Well, Nancy could just stick that in her pipe and smoke it. She was a little down right now (okay, maybe she was a lot down) but that didn't mean Violet had given up on life.

Did it?

She thought of Brian again, almost involuntarily. Their first date had been Chinese food and a long walk in the park. They'd talked and laughed like old friends all through dinner. As they'd walked together afterward, Brian had pointed out a cloud of fireflies and how they reflected in the rippling lake under the bridge. He'd reached for her hand then, and Violet had wished he'd never let go.

But that was before this last attack of her disease had finally damaged her ear canals so badly it couldn't be reversed. She would never hear Brian's soft, joyful laugh again. She would never again listen as he tuned his bass before a practice.

What musician would want to carry on a relationship with a deaf girl?

Sure, he kept texting her. Sure, he smiled at her and tried to talk to her when they met at the church. But that was probably because he felt obligated to. What kind of a jerk would stop seeing a girl because she went deaf?

Not a guy like Brian, that's for sure. So she'd made the hard decision for them both.

A hand landed on Violet's shoulder, and she felt herself shriek, even though she couldn't hear the sound she made. She turned so quickly she almost fell for the second time in one day, but strong hands caught her and held her up until her dizziness passed.

Nancy. Violet set her jaw and wondered if she should be angry that her friend was back again or if she should just hurry up and forgive her. Nancy had meant well, after all, even though she had been sneaky about it.

Violet decided on noncommittally sullen. "What do you want?"

Nancy held up a folded piece of paper for Violet to see. It was the same pamphlet Dr. Minelli had handed her earlier.

Let's go, Nancy mouthed.

Violet scowled. "Where? I'm trying to fix dinner right now."

Sign-language classes, Nancy said. *You need them. So do I.*

"Why do you need them?" Violet asked.

Nancy's dark eyes filled with tears. She blinked several times, probably to clear them. Violet's angry heart softened. *So I can talk to my best friend when she can't hear me anymore.*

Violet left her ingredients on the counter and took Nancy's arm to go outside. Nancy had left her car running and the passenger door open despite the late hour. That was just like her friend, to trust too much. If someone had stolen it, Nancy would say, *I guess they needed it more than I did.*

Violet had to smile. "You're lucky I live in a nice neighborhood."

Thanks to the headlights, it wasn't too dark to see Nancy's eyes roll.

*

The community college consisted of low buildings sprawled across a city block. The grounds were perfectly manicured expanses of lawn dotted with fountains and crisscrossed with broad paths. Even at this hour, it was lit up bright as day. Few people were around. Only the security guards in their motorized carts were visible. A youngish guard in the passenger seat waved and smiled. Nancy waved back, though Violet didn't.

Nancy picked a parking spot and led Violet into the nearest building. Inside, too, was brightly lit, and a group of people stood around in a lobby, talking and laughing. Violet's first instinct was to fall back away from them so they wouldn't try to talk to her. But on the edge, close to a classroom, a trio of young people signed excitedly to one another.

Violet stopped in her tracks. The brochure was right. Some of these happy people were deaf, too.

Their professor arrived a few minutes later. She was frazzled and wore glasses that were too big for her face, but she wrote her name on the chalk board with confident strokes. Dr. Porter, the board proclaimed. All of the chairs faced forward, so Dr. Porter could be clearly seen. Nancy and Violet took adjoining seats at the middle of the room and got down to business.

After class, while everyone was packing up their books and laptops, Dr. Porter wended her way through the desks to Violet and Nancy. She waved and gave them a friendly smile. As she introduced herself and welcomed them to the class, she mouthed all of her words clearly and signed as she spoke.

Tell me, Violet, she said, *how do you come to be learning ASL so late in life?*

Violet turned to Nancy, who gave her a supportive nod.

"I have Meniere's Disease," Violet said. "It effects the inner ear, so not only has my hearing been damaged past repair, but I also have vertigo and trouble with my balance. My doctor told me that the labyrinths in my ears have to be removed if I want to be able to walk again. She also gave me the brochure for this class. I wasn't going to come, but—" Violet shrugged—"Nancy insisted."

Dr. Porter smiled. *I'm so glad she did. For me, learning ASL was the turning point of my life. Before, I was shy and had trouble connecting with people. Now—*Dr. Porter paused to laugh—*it's impossible to shut me up. So to speak.*

Violet nodded. She wanted to laugh with the professor, but she just couldn't. Not today. "So you learned ASL later in life as well?"

Dr. Porter's fluent fingers continued to fly as she mouthed, *Yes. I lost my hearing in an accident about fifteen years ago. I spent roughly a year struggling through relationships in which I couldn't communicate. But then one day I decided I'd spent enough time feeling sorry for myself. I needed to be the change I wanted to see, as they say.*

"I admire your bravery," Violet told her. "I'm not sure if I'll ever get to the point where I'll be happy again. I'm a pianist and a singer, and I found out today that I'll never hear another piece of music, let alone perform one."

Dr. Porter reached out to place a comforting hand on Violet's shoulder. She had to break the touch before she could go on. *This is very fresh for you, and I can't blame you for being unsure how you'll go on. But if I may offer some unsolicited advice, I'd like to remind you that Beethoven was deaf toward the end of his life.*

"Right," Violet agreed. "He composed Ode to Joy when he could no longer hear the orchestra. But I'm not a genius. I'm just a worship leader at my church."

Dr. Porter smiled, gently and sadly. *It's not his ability to compose without his hearing that I'd like you to emulate. It's his refusal to give up.*

Like you said, he wrote Ode to Joy while he was deaf. That isn't a piece of music composed by a man who has forgotten that life is worth living.

Violet found that she couldn't respond. She was suddenly overcome by shame. *Oh, Lord,* she thought. *I've forgotten how beautiful life can be, haven't I? I've forgotten to be grateful.*

Dr. Porter patted Violet's shoulder again. *I hope to see you Wednesday, Violet.*

"You will," Violet said, and she meant it.

*

ASL class was on Monday and Wednesday, and Nancy picked Violet up for it every time. They sat together and practiced together, signing slowly and clearly to help each other pick it up. It was a small step, and learning a new language was difficult, but the class made Violet feel hopeful for the first time since she'd found out she might lose her hearing. Maybe she'd have to learn a new career, but at least she had friends who cared enough to break through the silence.

The day before her surgery, Nancy offered to stay home and eat ice cream with Violet instead of going to class, but Violet decided to go anyway. She wanted the moral support of friendly classmates and her understanding professor. She didn't expect to see a giant bouquet of spring flowers with a card signed by everyone in her ASL class.

She found that evening that she could still sign with tears in her eyes: *Thank you all. This means so much to me.*

She and Nancy carried the flowers out after class, and Violet fervently prayed that she wouldn't drop them and break the vase. When Nancy stopped short, she almost toppled over.

Don't look now, Nancy signed, *but we have company.*

Violet followed Nancy's gaze. Brian sat at one of the tables in the lobby, eating a sandwich and studying a textbook. He still wore his leather jacket despite the warmth of the room. A pair of wire-rimmed reading glasses Violet had never seen before perched delicately on the bridge of his nose. Her heart clenched hard. Even in glasses, looking out of place in this tweedy setting, he was still gorgeous. She had almost managed to stop missing him until right now.

He's taking classes here? Violet signed. *What for?*

Nancy shrugged. *Should we talk to him, or just keep walking?*

She thought of the last time she'd seen him, when she'd pitched head-over-heels and he'd had to pick her up. Violet's cheeks burned with embarrassment.

Keep walking, Violet signed. She lifted the flowers up to cover her still-red face and they left through the opposite door.

*

The surgery went exactly as it was supposed to, and Violet woke up inside a shroud of silence thick as a building's foundation. She'd been prepared for it, but it still hit her hard enough to knock her into bed for a week. Nancy came every day to make sure Violet was eating and to bring her the homework from their class. She signed to Nancy that her head hurt (it did) to make sure Nancy let her stay in bed, but of all her post-surgery aches, it was her heart that hurt the worst.

It was seven o'clock on Tuesday evening when she woke up from a pain-pill induced sleep to the strains of Bach playing through her head. She lay in bed in the early evening gloom, staring at the ceiling. There was a time, not long ago, when she could play that song from memory. Could she still do it? The keys would feel the same, even if she couldn't hear them.

Violet lifted herself slowly out of bed, but the dizziness didn't hit her as immediately as usual. In fact, as she re-gained her feet, she realized she could stand without her feet slipping out from under her.

She made her way into the living room and sat down on the piano bench. She positioned her hands in the old, familiar way and began to play. She couldn't hear a note of it. But the muscle memory was still there, and if she thought of it, she could remember the sound of this piece she loved so much.

It wasn't much, but it was something. Her music wasn't gone. It was just different.

A hand landed on her shoulder and she shrieked. Behind her, Brian stood with his hands in the air to show their emptiness.

I'm sorry, he mouthed, while her heart still pounded against her ribcage. Then he brought his hands together and signed, *I'm sorry. I'm sorry I startled you. I texted you that I was coming over, but you didn't respond.*

For a moment, she was too stunned to do anything but hold her hands against her chest. What was he doing here? Had Nancy forgotten to lock the door when she left this afternoon? Oh, Lord, how did her hair look? She hadn't taken a shower in two days.

But the question she asked was, *When did you learn how to sign?*

Brian flushed with embarrassment and he signed back, *I've been taking a class at the community college. It seems like some of the people I like the best can't hear very well these days.*

Did he—did he mean her? Violet stood. Brian reached out to steady her, but she was firm on her feet. She gestured to her couch and signed, *Won't you sit down?*

Brian gave her that familiar, beautiful smile and did as she directed. She joined him there on the cushion.

You sound great, he signed. *Just as nice as ever.*

Violet shrugged. *It's strange not to be able to hear my own playing.*

Brian's smile faded. *I can imagine. Hey, I brought you something, but I left it in my car. I'll be right back.*

She waited for him to return, watching the door so he wouldn't have to touch her shoulder again. He re-appeared a few moments later with a box, which he placed beside her on the couch.

It's a door light, he signed. *Nancy said that you can't hear the doorbell and that she often startles you when she comes to visit. I found this online and—*he shrugged. *It seems like a really easy way to solve a problem.*

She wasn't sure how to process all of this. *How thoughtful,* she signed. *I don't know what to say.*

Brian grinned again. *I'll set it up. Just give me a second.*

He bustled around her house, from door to computer to back again. She had never realized, when she could hear his voice, how gracefully he moved. Had he studied dance? And how had she managed to work with him for an entire year without noticing how those long hands were good for more than teasing out a bassline?

When he was finished, he placed a white square of plastic on her piano and gestured for her to stay still. He ran around to the front door again, and suddenly the thing flashed a pulsing light.

Brian came back in smiling. Violet smiled back and signed, *It works great! Thank you!*

It's so great to see you smiling, Brian signed. *Last time you smiled at me like this was when I held your hand that night at the park. Do you remember that? We were walking over the bridge, looking at the fireflies.*

I remember, Violet signed. Oh, why had she let him stay? She knew what he felt for her, and she'd let him into her life again anyway. What did it matter if she felt the same way? She could never have a real relationship with Brian when she knew how important music was to him. Hesitantly, she signed, *Brian, look.*

He held up a hand to stop her. *Don't worry. You told me you don't have space in your life for a romantic relationship. I totally understand that. But I care about you, Violet. I just want to be in your life in whatever way you'll let me. If that's just as your friend, then that's what I'll be.*

Her heart swelled. Why, oh why did he have to be so good? If he was some pushy jerk who just wanted his own way, she would throw him out of her house and never set eyes on him again. But this? How could she turn away the friendship of so good a man?

It's not that I don't care about you. It's just that it would never work out with us. How could somebody with your musical talent be with a deaf girl? It just doesn't make sense.

Brian reached out and took both of her hands in his. Very slowly, very clearly, he mouthed, *None of that matters to me, Violet. Whether you can hear me or not, you understand what's in my heart. And I understand what's in yours. Most people who can hear each other don't have that much going for them.*

"Brian, I—" she could feel the words in her mouth, but she couldn't hear them at all. She gave up. What was the point?

He let go of her hands and stood up. *Like I said,* he signed, *I'm your friend. Hey, if you feel up to it, you should come to service on Sunday. The band and I have a surprise for you.*

I'll see what I can do, Violet signed. She walked Brian to the door and shut it behind him.

*

Saturday night, Violet couldn't sleep. She tossed and turned in her bed, watching the shadows change on her ceiling. *The band has a surprise for me,* she thought. *Randy and Lisa and whoever it is they picked to replace me.* Brian too, of course. Brian, who understood what was in her heart. Who was convinced she understood what was in his. Brian, who said he wanted to be her friend but smiled at her in a way that made her feel like the only woman on earth. Brian, who had learned to sign when she could no longer hear his voice.

There would be other people there, too. There would be people she had known for years but would no longer be able to speak to. There would be people who would want to know why she hadn't showed her face in church for such a long time. What would she say to them? *Well, I'm deaf now. I can't hear the sermon.* Or maybe even, *God has forgotten me, so now I'm busy forgetting him.* What was old Mrs. Jenkins going to say to that? She would definitely not look kindly on a crisis of faith from a person who'd been a worship leader. Nobody understood what it was like for her to be cut off from music. It was like she'd died.

Why, Lord? She thought. *Why did You let this happen to me? Why would You give me this musical ability and then take it away?*

A still, small voice inside of her answered, *Sometimes, you can't see what's really important until you clear out what isn't.*

As those words ran through her head like a mantra, Violet was finally able to fall asleep.

She woke the next morning without benefit of an alarm clock and took her shower. Violet chose her clothes carefully, curled her hair, and applied her make-up with a steady hand.

Well, she couldn't hear, but she sure looked good.

She hadn't yet fixed her car up with the interior signals she would need to drive, so Nancy picked her up. She grinned hugely and threw her arms around Violet in a tight hug.

The church parking lot was full of shiny cars and happy people wearing their best clothes. When she got out of the car, Mr. Hernandez hurried over. He spoke quickly, and Violet frowned. Nancy stopped him with a touch on his arm, and Mr. Hernandez stopped talking, turned to face Violet directly, and mouthed, *It's so good to see you, Violet. We've all really missed you.*

As she made her way inside, it seemed as if everyone had missed her. She found that she'd really missed them, too. All this time that she'd been holed up in her house, leaving it only for doctor's appointments and ASL classes, she hadn't realized how thin and attenuated her spirit had become. But when these people hugged her, they fed her soul. She felt lifted, and fulfilled, and very, very loved.

Pastor found her in the lobby before she sat down. *Violet!* He mouthed. *I'm so glad to see you! Can you stick around after the service to talk? I have an idea about how we can keep you on your insurance.*

That would be amazing, Violet replied.

Brian, Lisa, and Randy weren't around, but she wasn't surprised. They would be backstage, preparing their music and warming up their voices. They might even be prepping the new keyboard player, depending how long they'd been together. She sat with Nancy in the front row of the nave where it would be easy to read Pastor's lips when he talked. What she didn't catch, Nancy translated into sign for her.

Nancy had to translate, *I'd like to welcome our worship team to the stage now. They have a very special presentation they've prepared for a member of our congregation. Let's hear it!*

A blaze of light kicked on, bright white as the sun, and the band swaggered out onto the stage. Lisa waved and picked up her microphone. Randy followed her, then a woman Violet didn't know who took up residence behind the keyboard, and finally, Brian sauntered out in his leather jacket, grinning. He waved at Violet, who waved back. Her stomach flipped twice. It was almost ridiculous how good-looking he was.

The lights strobed yellow, then green, like the footlights in a rock show. Instead of holding up his bass, Brian took a section of stage next to Lisa. When Randy started to strum and Lisa took up her mic, Brian signed, *This is for you, Violet. You don't have to listen to understand my heart.*

Nancy shot her a sly, sideways smile, but Violet couldn't take the time to pay attention to her. The lights at the bottom of the stage weren't the only ones—the ceiling had been strung with fairy lights, and these flashed in rhythm, changing colors and sparkling against the dimmed lights of the nave. Lisa raised her mic to her lips and began to sing. Beside her, Brian signed the words to a worship song they had sung together a thousand times. In her memory, the sound of his sweet baritone spiraling with her own toward heaven was so strong she could almost hear it. She could feel the presence of God Almighty more strongly than she had in months. Tears stung her eyes and raced down her cheeks. *Sometimes, you can't see what's really important until you clear out the rest.*

*

After the service, Brian found Violet in the lobby. Nancy squeezed her hand and moved away to talk to someone else, leaving her alone with the handsome bass player.

What did you think? Brian signed.

Violet had been wondering what she would say to him ever since his set ended. There had been so many things racing through her mind then. But now, in this moment, all she could manage was, *I don't think anyone has ever done something like this for me. It was so beautiful.*

Brian smiled. *I got the idea from the doorbell I brought you. I thought, she may not be able to hear anymore, but that isn't the only way to experience music.*

Violet wrapped her arms around his shoulders and went up on her tiptoes. She kissed his mouth very softly, like a promise. Brian slid his arms around her waist and held her against him. He said nothing. He didn't need to.

Someone tapped her shoulder, and Violet turned. Pastor stood behind her, smiling knowingly. Brian let her go so suddenly she almost stumbled, but she caught herself on his shoulder before she could.

Pastor said, *I was thinking, your insurance won't be cancelled if you still work here. The church sure could bring in a lot more parishioners if we had a full-time ASL translator.*

For the second time that Sunday morning, tears filled Violet's eyes. *I hear You, Lord,* she thought. *I hear You loud and clear.*

AN ANGEL TO WATCH OVER ME

NATALIE MEYER

Chapter 1

The pulsing rhythm of the music vibrated against the walls and the stale smoked filled air of the club was something Willow had become accustomed to since her slippery slide into rebellion. Other than by association one would never have thought she was the minister's daughter. But that is exactly what brought her here. For years she pretended to be the prim and proper Willow Leandra Dawson, playing the piano in church and volunteering to feed the hungry. But as she grew older she started to see how the church was run by politics and rich people.

To her it was an absolute farce, with a bunch of phonies claiming to know the answer to eternity. On her sixteenth birthday she had enough, when she asked her father if she could have a dance party like all the other teens her age. Instead he gave her the speech about fornication and the Ten Commandments. The turning point came when one of the assisting ministers conveniently started an affair and the church simply swept it all under the carpet, hiding the dirty secret like they hid so many others. If anyone could tell the world what goes on behind the scenes of a church, the minister's children could.

"Willow, want another one?" Dustin asked over the noise and flopped down beside her.

"Yeah sure, keep them coming," she said and held her glass out to Dustin.

She knew that she will be regret everything in the morning when she woke up with a hangover, but that was a bridge she would cross in the morning, and it's not as if her parents would know. Granted, she was already twenty-two and living on her own, she tried not to provoke her father and upset her mother. So she made sure that when she did visit them she portrayed pure innocence. What they didn't know wouldn't hurt them.

Rob dropped down next to her and he held out a rolled up joint, "You look like you need some."

One thing Willow never indulged in was drugs, she would drink until the sun came up and party for weeks on end, but she had made one promise and that is to never touch drugs. An overdose cost her brother his life about seven years ago. He was much older than her when he died, and that was part and parcel of why she hated the church so much and why she despised her dad. They knew he had issues, but they turned a blind eye, pretended that there was nothing wrong. Whenever Marcus got in trouble, her dad would bail him out and then they would ship him off to some rehab center and make lengthy excuses that he was being treated for some mental disorder. No one ever knew, and the only reason Willow knew was because she was always caught in the middle of the fallouts when Marcus and her dad went at each other's throats.

"No thanks, I've had my share," she said and pushed herself up from the sofa. She stumbled a few feet and then leaned against one of the pillars in her intoxicated state. She just needed some fresh air and then she would be on her way home.

She stumbled out into the alley and clutched her coat tighter around her waist to keep warm, her phone vibrated in her pocket and at first she ignored it, but when it carried on she cursed under her breath and took it out.

"This better be good," she slurred and leaned against the wall.

"Miss Thomson?"

"Yes?"

"Uh, we need you to come to Angels Memorial hospital, there's been an accident."

"I'm sorry, what?"

"Angels Memorial, there's been an accident and we need you to get here as soon as you can."

The line crackled and then the call died. Her battery was dead, but she suddenly felt sober. With no detail on what was going on, panic wrapped its icy claw around her heart and she immediately flagged a cab down.

"Angels Memorial please," she said and rested back against the seat.

What could possibly have happened and why are they calling her to come to the hospital. She tried to turn her phone back on but each time it started up it shut down straight away.

"Stupid phone," she grunted and tossed it in her bag.

Angels Memorial came into sight and as expected several ambulances with their red flashing lights stood lined up outside the ER. She paid the cab fare and hurried out of the cab and towards the hospital.

To get information from reception was another story, people were crowding the place, pushing and shoving each other in the line.

"Excuse me," she said and pulled on one of the nurse's coats, "Someone called me to come to the hospital urgently. My name is Willow Dawson."

"Willow?" a familiar voice drew her attention; it was one of the church deacons.

"Deacon Roland... they called me to come to the ER," she said as the feeling of dread consumed her.

"I'm so sorry sweetheart, but your mom and dad..." he choked up and cleared his throat, "There was a terrible accident, and they tried everything to save them..."

"What do you mean them? Where are my mom and dad!" she said anxiously.

"They didn't make it; we tried to get a hold of you as soon as we heard that they were brought here, but..."

"You're lying!" She cried out and rushed straight into the ER, "I'm looking for Mr. and Mrs. Dawson!" she called out but it seemed like no-one was listening. Everyone was rushing past her back and forth, calling out instructions and attending to patients lying in gurneys.

A doctor came rushing past but she grabbed him by his sleeve, "Mr. Dawson, I need to see Mr. Dawson."

He stopped and pulled her aside, and then the Deacon came to stand beside her and placed his hand on her shoulder, but she shrugged away from him.

"Miss Dawson, let's step into the family room," he said calmly but by the tone of his voice she realized that something terrible had happened.

The doctor and Deacon Roland walked with her and when she finally reached the family room she slumped down in one of the chairs and looked up at both men standing before her.

"Willow, can I get you some coffee?" the Deacon offered.

She looked up at him and through clenched teeth said, "No, I don't want coffee, I want to see my parents."

He stood there in silence with his head bowed, and the doctor stepped forward.

"Miss Dawson this is not easy and I wish I had better news, but earlier this evening both your mother and father had succumbed to their injuries following a car accident. I'm truly sorry."

Deacon Roland knelt down in front of her and touched her hand.

"They're gone Willow, they were on their way back from prayer meeting when a construction vehicle plowed into them at an intersection. You're mom died on the impact and your dad succumbed to his injuries here in the ER."

Her entire body went cold as she felt herself slip into this black hole of grief and desolation. This cannot be, they cannot be dead. It's enough that she had lost her brother, now her mom and dad too. Where does that leave her?

She sunk to her knees and let out a loud agonizing cry and tears flowed freely down her cheeks, her entire life and everything she knew lost. The pain that raided her heart and soul was almost too much to bear, she wanted to die.

"Willow, Maggie said you can come and stay with us if you'd like.

Between the sobs and cries, she didn't hear a word anyone was saying, all she knew was that her end was near and now that she had nothing to live for, she might as well make an end to it.

Even as the Deacon led her out of the ER, her feet felt heavy and her heart felt dead, everything inside her felt like led being pulled down by the force of gravity and all she wanted was to lay down and never get up.

Chapter 2

Willow stood at the graves of her parents, somehow even the heavens mirrored her sorrow as the rain poured down, drenching the earth with its tears and as she watched their caskets being lowered into the earth where they will forever lay, her heart sank with them. Nothing and no-one could comfort her since there was nothing left to comfort. Only a black empty soul of the woman she once was.

As the last of the people who came to pay their respect left, she stayed behind and sunk to her knees. Her tears had already dried up and all that was left was the extreme emptiness she felt.

"Why did you have to go?" she asked softly, "You weren't supposed to die; you promised me you will always be there for me."

The longer she sat like that in the mud next to their graves the angrier she became. She had gotten over the denial of her loss, spent days mourning their death and now a deep dark rage that stirred her soul slowly started to rise up inside of her like a tornado out for destruction.

She slammed her hand into the mud and dug her fingers into the soft soil, then let out a loud agonizing cry, "You took them from me! They believed in you, and you let them down, show yourself God, if you are in the least bit concerned about us you will show yourself!" And as she ran out of breath and her voice strained she slumped forward and sobbed.

Who was she kidding, she never believed in a higher power, and this proved her point. Life was nothing but a play script performed on the greatest stage of all for the universe to laugh at and for the Creator's entertainment.

Willow raised her head and looked at the tombstones that stuck out of the ground above the open graves that gaped open before her, on her mother's stone was written – Three things will last forever - faith, hope, and love. And the greatest of these is love. 1 Cor 13v13 – even to the end her mother and father were blinded by this fake faith they clung to, she thought bitterly before she crawled out of the rain to find shelter next to a mausoleum adorned with two weeping angels. She simply couldn't bring herself to leave their sides, not just yet.

****

Raquel soared through the skies above the earthly realm and although he was reduced to the status of a guardian angel, he counted himself lucky that he was never banished to the acrid fires of Seoul like the rest of the rebels who opposed the Father. At least he still had his wings, and although his purpose was much lesser than what he was initially created for, he still had some hope to redeem himself.

Raquel spiraled upwards, as high as his wings would take him and then with one single beat forward he slowed himself down to a complete halt. He felt an unfamiliar tug in his being followed by a distant voice. He stood suspended high above the earth with the universe as his backdrop and the stars like silent witnesses surrounding him.

Someone was calling his name, and it was a voice that sounded like a Seraphs melodic tone, but it wasn't coming from heaven. It was coming from earth. He narrowed his gaze in on the earth and slowly descended, trying to determine where the call is coming from, and the closer the got the clearer her voice became. An unexpected gust of wind swirled around him and cast him downward, and in that instant he realized he had been called upon. As he dove lower he flew across the waters that covered the earth and for the first time he felt the warmth of the yellow star dance across his wings. His sapphire eyes searched for his sired soul, the one who called for his protection and guidance. And as he soared further through changing seasons he finally reached a patch of ground filled with lost roaming souls, the souls of the damned and those caught in between. Among the souls he spotted the lone figure curled up between two weeping angels and as he approached her, the rain parted in front of him like a curtain until he slowly descended to the ground. Never reveal your true self, his conscience reminded him and he quickly tucked his wings away before he crouched down beside the woman.

What would he even say to her? He wondered as he hesitated to speak. From what he knew, mortals were not that forthcoming to strangers least of all those who fall from the sky unannounced. He would have to rethink his approach he realized as he turned invisible to the naked eye. He was going to follow her and find the opportune moment to introduce himself and instead of entertaining himself by scaring the poor soul to death, he moved back and sat across from her.

It was amazing how time is such an insignificant concept up there among the stars, while here on this mortal plane, time is all they have. A time to live and a time to die, a time to love and a time to hate, the very words the Father spoke into the heart of the great King Solomon. He never quite understood it, but now here where he sat, it was slowly starting to dawn on him. He stood up and paced before her, wondering if she will ever rise from her slumber and he was about to rest his hand on her shoulder when she finally pushed herself up from the cold stone floor.

She looked broken and torn, her raven black hair clung to her cheeks and a black substance ran down from her eyes over her cheeks. Surely his Father will not assign him to a demon? He moved closer and crouched down before her, his nose almost touching hers and behind the veil of black tears, he saw her emerald colored eyes. She looked straight at him and stood up unaware of his presence and then stepped down the small stair and walked straight through him. And the moment she did that he felt an immense force of power course through every fiber of his being.

"Extraordinary," he said to himself as he fell into step next to the mortal woman.

He could sense the intense sorrow that radiated from her and he couldn't help but wonder what it was that darkened her soul so much.

It would have been handy if every mortal came with a how-I-work manual or some form of instruction guide; he thought and rolled his neck. He should have paid more attention to the others and tried to at least seem interested in what they had to deal with.

Chapter 3

Willow walked hurriedly along the quite road to her apartment, the whole time it felt as if something or someone was watching her. She clutched her drenched coat tighter around her and walked ahead with her head hung low. Was it possible that her parents' spirits were following her?

As she passed the small Hungarian bakery on the corner of Sixth and Hampshire Avenue she glanced at her reflection in the window and stopped dead in her tracks. Behind her stood a taller than average man and she was sure that there was no-one with her a moment ago. Her heart started racing and too afraid to turn she closed her eyes and opened them again only to find the tall man with the sapphire blue eyes standing next to her. He looked at her with an intensity that made her feel almost insignificant.

"You can see me," he said in a deep timber voice filled with wonder.

Willow frowned and shoved past him, "You're a nut case get away from me."

"Pardon me?" he said and fell into step beside her, "What is a nut case?"

"Are you kidding me?"

"I'm afraid I do not understand what you mean," the stranger said again and Willow picked up her pace. But all of a sudden everything around her stood still as if suspended in time and space. Even the water pouring from a broken gutter hung like weightless droplets in mid-air.

"Wh-what's going on?" she asked nervously as she looked around her.

"Why are you running away from me?" he asked.

She looked around her and glanced at the reflection of a window then whipped her head back and looked at the stranger, "What are you?"

"You called for me; surely you know what my purpose is."

"I-I never... what do you mean I called for you and why do you have wings?"

None of this made sense, before her stood a man with eyes like amethysts, a violet intense color that was almost hypnotic, and hair the color of an overcast sky. He was by far the most beautiful man she had ever encountered and to make him near perfect he had wings that expanded on either side of him and they glowed like the moon hidden behind a curtain of fog.

"You called for your Guardian, I'm sired to serve and protect you."

"What, are you insane?" she laughed incredulously, but the expression on his face was deadly serious.

She covered her hands over her ears and closed her eyes. This was all a dream and none of this was real, she kept saying to herself, in the hope that once she opened her eyes, the stranger would be gone. Instead of waiting to see if he was still here, she spun around and started to run, but he appeared next to her as if floating weightlessly in the air.

"Stop that!" she said and shoved against him mid-running, but he simply swept her up into his arms and spiraled upwards until they were high above the buildings. When he finally descended they were standing on the roof of one of the high-rises overlooking the city, and down below life started to move as normal.

"You have little faith mortal, my name is Raquel and I have been appointed as your guardian angel."

She laughed and shook her head in utter disbelief, "My guardian angel, are you serious?"

His blue eyes burned into her soul and she curiously stepped forward, "Okay then, if you are what you say you are, fine, but you can't go walking around with-with those things flapping behind you."

In a flash of light, Raquel's wings disappeared and he stood before her dressed in black. This had to be her imagination playing tricks on her, she thought as she studied the man. She tried to remember what she learned in church, tried to recall stories of guardian angels, but none of them matched what she was experiencing. Maybe it wouldn't be all that bad having a guardian angel as company, even if it was her imagination, she thought.

"I have rules," she started, still perplexed by what was happening.

"Slap me," he said.

"Slap you?" she asked tilting her head.

"Yes, slap me."

"Uh... all right then," Willow stepped forward and slapped Raquel in the face, which against all odds took him by surprise

"Why would you be so violent," he asked touching his cheek.

"You asked me to slap you."

"I meant to say, share your rules with me? As in slap me, is that one a term used by mortals often?"

Willow suddenly burst out laughing, "Oh wait, you meant to say hit me."

"Is that not the same?"

"No!" she said as she clutched her stomach, "You sure you want to spend your days tending to a broken mortal?" she giggled.

"You are indeed complex creatures," Raquel said with his hands clasped in front of him, "You said you had rules?"

"Never mind the rules, I just need to get home and get some sleep so that I can put this entire day behind me."

"Very well," Raquel said and reached to take her into his arms but she quickly pushed against his chest.

"I'll take the elevator, thanks."

Raquel followed her in silence the rest of the way, and Willow couldn't help but wonder just how much of her mind had taken a temporary leave of absence.

Chapter 4

Raquel was quite transfixed on the mortal's way of life, her home was in disarray and the complete opposite of what he was used to, but even in this chaos he found a mysterious sense of beauty that captivated him. He soon learned that the woman's name was Willow, but of her woes he could only make his own assumptions. She had lost someone dear to her, and she was struggling to come to terms with her loss. Considering the fact that he found her curled up on holy ground among restless souls also pointed that out

"Why were you in the cemetery?" he asked as he walked around her apartment.

"Dancing," she said.

He looked at her quizzically, "Why?"

"Ugh, I was attending a funeral, if you're an angel, aren't you supposed to know everything?"

Raquel tilted his head to the side and for the first time dared to smile, "I'm an angel, not God. We are more than mortals, but far less that our Father."

"Ah, omnipresent, I suppose that makes sense," she said as she started to pick up her clothes that lay scattered across the floor.

Raquel couldn't help but notice the way her hair swooped forward like a heavy black curtain whenever she bent down. Out of the blue, he had the urge to reach out and touch the silky tresses that tempted him.

"Cake?" she suddenly spoke pulling him out of his trance, "It's all I have at the moment."

"What is it?" he asked and scrutinized the dark brown sponge-like substance she reached for and held out to him.

"You eat it, that's what mortals do," she said and raised the piece of cake towards his mouth, but instead of avoiding eminent collision with a piece of mortal food that smelled like cocoa and vanilla, he opened his mouth and took a bite.

"Mmm," he said and as the cake melted on his tongue.

"Now I know why our Father warned us about gluttony, you mortals can so easily fall prey to these insignificant temptations."

"It's what makes us human," she said, "Those insignificant temptations we get to turn down or embrace, because we can make those choices. It's called free will, a term I'm sure you must have heard about before."

Her voice faded as she left the room Raquel was in but he didn't follow her, instead he studied the books that were lined on the shelves, most of which had gathered dust over the years. He also felt a need to put a safer distance between himself and the mortal all of a sudden.

There was something terribly wrong, he suddenly felt out of control and the same desire that cost him his place in heaven was now knocking at the door, but instead of the need to be an equal to the Father it now came in the form of a mortal woman and he wanted her. He was well aware of the fact that they too had rules when descending to this realm, and so far he had broken each one as if they were meant to be broken.

First, he reveals himself to the mortal woman, then he eats a substance that may have bewitched him and now he felt like he was caught in his own version of the Songs of Solomon, a book all too familiar to every single angel from the heavens down to the fiery pits of hell. He took a deep breath and exhaled, and as he did his breath kicked up a cloud of dust that spiraled into the air and slowly descended and settled back down on the books. He needed to find out from his brothers if any of them ever felt as tempted as he felt this very moment.

He walked over to the window and unfurled his wings, and with one glance back into the directly his sired soul disappeared, he launched himself up into the air and ascended until he was well out of reach of the intoxicating scent that kept tormenting him.

"Raquel, back so soon?" Lysander said beside him.

"Just getting some distance from that forsaken world."

"I warned you that creation was all but perfect, have you seen how some of those mortals conduct themselves? It's shameless."

"It's not that, it's my sired soul, she…"

"Oh look who's being tempted," Daniel, one of the other angels called out as he descended down to join Raquel and Lysander, "It's not easy to stay chaste is it?"

"I do not know what you're talking about," Raquel ground out as he hovered above the clouds.

"Denial is such a weak trait," Daniel said and chuckled.

This was not helping him in the least bit, he realized and he grew more and more restless the longer he was away from Willow. Being too close to her was tempting and being too far from her was weakening. However, was he going to manage this task without failing?

Chapter 5

It's been two weeks since the stranger walked into her life and then disappeared into thin air without saying a word. And with every passing day, she started to realize more and more that the whole thing might have just been a figment of her imagination. It may have seemed real at the time, but in her state of mind, anything would have been possible. Yet, every now and again she could feel his presence, the same sensation she felt when she first realized she was being followed or he had just gotten better at hiding. What was even more puzzling was that she had distanced herself from her so-called friends and even the smell or taste of alcohol made her feel sick. Somewhere between then and now she managed to sober up without consciously trying. She had even taken out the bible her mother gave her in an attempt to find peace, but she was yet to turn the first page.

Like most days, she found herself sitting on the windowsill as she looked out over the city, wondering what her mother and father did on their last night, and whether or not they were in a good place. She was almost certain that they were ready for whatever waited on the other side. It was a comforting notion, but a daunting one. She couldn't help but wonder what it would be like if she had to look death right in the eyes. Would death sweep down on a gentle breeze of peace and tranquillity and simply whisk her soul away, or will he come with his armies and drag her from this world kicking and screaming.

"You think too much about what could have been."

Raquel's disembodied voice sounded like a soothing melody in her ear.

"You're back," she said softly and let out a sigh, "I was starting to think you were a figment of my imagination."

"I never left," he said and then only made himself visible to her.

"Well you weren't here either, so do you have more than one person to look after at a time?" she asked and swung her legs down from the windowsill and lowered them to the floor.

"Only you," he stepped closer and she could see the confusion flash in his eyes.

"Why are you looking at me like that?" she asked tentatively.

"You remind me of heaven," he whispered as he raised his hand almost as if to reach out to her.

She felt a blush creep into her skin and she bit her lip nervously, "You're acting all strange, you're supposed to be the one in control."

"Easier said than done," his fingertips finally brushed her cheek and she felt a jolt of static electricity ricochet through her body.

"Is-Isn't this sort of thing against the rules? Wasn't this why some of you were thrown out of heaven?" she stuttered but was incapable of moving, it was as if some magnetic force was pulling her towards him.

"I'm in a state of purgatory, I'm not in heaven and I'm not in hell. All of us are in limbo waiting for souls that need our guidance. The Arch Angels and the Seraphs are up high, with the Father, while we... we wait for absolution."

Willow's eyes shot full of tears, not for her own pain but for his. Although he was an angel he was no different than her, he was as lost as she was. She stepped closer and reached up to touch his cheek, but as she did she felt the presence of a different entity and at that very moment Raquel also took a step away.

"Why isn't this cozy?"

Willow turned towards the sound of an unfamiliar voice, it was another man, much like Raquel but not as handsome who appeared out of nowhere, but he didn't seem to even grant her a second look.

"You know very well that the sin you are about to commit is punishable by eternal banishment Raquel, are you willing to be so foolish?" the man said and Willow felt a chill run down her spine, she had to do something.

"Excuse me," Willow said and stepped forward.

The angel held his breath and looked down at her.

"She can see and hear you Lysander," Raquel said with a smirk.

"How is that possible?" He asked and bent forward scrutinizing her with his deep blue gaze. He looked so similar but yet so different to Raquel, same color eyes, and cloud gray hair.

"I don't know how it is possible, but I do," Willow said and tilted her chin defiantly; "Now please tell me what's going on?"

"I believe Raquel will have to tell you the truth, my work here is done," Lysander said and turned to Raquel, "Don't be foolish brother. It's not worth losing everything you worked so hard for."

A gush of wind whipped through the apartment and then the angel named Lysander was gone.

Willow turned to Raquel and crossed her arms, "What was he trying to say? I thought that you said you're in between heaven and hell, which means you technically belong nowhere in particular."

Raquel walked over to the window and rested his forearm above him against the window frame.

"It's complicated. When the uprising happened and Lucifer was cast out along with his followers, some of us were faced with indecision. We refused to take either part, so, we were banished but our sins were not like those of Lucifer and his hordes," Raquel turned and looked at Willow, "We are most intimately involved with the Fathers' creation, and as a result we also start to sense and feel what they feel, some are stronger than others, but in essence we get tempted. And once we fall for temptation, we will be lost to heaven for eternity."

"So if you're a good angel you can still go to heaven?" Willow asked curiously.

"You could say that," Raquel said and sighed. "You're a temptation for me, and Lysander came to bring me to my senses."

Willow bit her lip and pinched the bridge of her nose, although he made it sound like temptation was a bad thing, she couldn't help but feel a sense of excitement rush through her. In the same breath, she was not sure if she would want to be the cause for Raquel to be banished from heaving for eternity.

She turned to Raquel and sighed, "I relieve you from your duties."

His laughter echoed through the apartment and she frowned at him, "It's not funny, I'm not going to be responsible for your downfall."

Raquel stepped closer and twisted a strand of her hair around his finger, "If only it was that easy."

She leaned into his touch and closed her eyes, and then he was gone.

Chapter 6

A year later...

Willow finally decided to take control of her life again. She found work at a day care center in a small town teaching pre-schoolers and had taken up studying to become a full time teacher. It had always been her dream, but she just never followed through. Now everything had finally fallen into place and for the first time in her life, she felt she had a purpose and to see children play and smile was more rewarding than anything.

"Miss Dawson! Miss Dawson! Please tell us the story about the angels?" little Zoey piped up.

She had created her own story of Guardian Angels, and although it was a little fabricated from her own experience, it was her way to stay connected to Raquel's memory, wherever he found himself.

She never blamed him for leaving, and as much as it hurt at first, she knew that she did the right thing, and somewhere out there he was being what he was destined to be, a guardian angel to another distraught person who needed him.

"First we need to do your ABC's," Willow said as she handed out blank sheets of paper, "and then I will tell you all about the guardian angels that live among us."

The kids all cheered and as they settled down for the lesson, there was a slight knock on the classroom's door.

"Miss Dawson," the principal said as she entered the classroom, "I'm so sorry to interrupt your lesson, but I just wanted to introduce everyone to the new deputy principal."

Willow smiled, "Of course. Please stand up children," she said turning her attention to her class, but as the new deputy principal entered the classroom he stole her breath away. Raquel.

"Children, this is Deputy Principle Eduard Raquel, he will be joining us from today, and let's welcome him."

In unison the children all welcomed him while Willow stood frozen on the spot, unable to say a word, and all Raquel did was smile and wink at her.

Much later during break time he joined Willow on the playground.

"I told you it was easier said than done," he said and smiled.

"I told you it was not worth the sacrifice," she said, too afraid to look at him and expose her inner feelings.

He casually linked his fingers with hers and turned her to face him, "You are worth the sacrifice, you reminded me too much of heaven, and I could no longer stay away."

She looked up at him and smiled, "Does this mean you're staying for good?"

"Indefinitely."

~The End~

BONUS STORY:

The train screeched to a halt and Elaine Sheldon had to brace herself for the onslaught of people trying to squeeze past out. Holding tightly around the handrail, she winced when a rushing man bumped his laptop bag against her hips, and she took a few steps back with the impact.

The man did not stop to apologize and Elaine only heaved a sigh and fixed her stance as the train resumed moving.

It was supposed to be a five-minute walk from the station to her apartment, but tonight, it did not feel like it. Her steps were slow and her shoulders were drooped. The streetlights refused to turn on properly and it flickered repeatedly as she passed by. Elaine sighed at the dreary atmosphere.

Just a week ago, these walks home passed by with a spring in her step, looking forward to the person who was waiting for her to be back, the person she had been going home to for the past six months, the man who welcomed her with a warm hug and a big smile after a tiring day at work—until the other day.

Her eyes felt heavy and the long wait for the elevator was not helping with her mood. She watched as the red arrow went down as minutes passed by until it reached the ground floor. Her ride back up was spent alone. She smiled bitterly. The world must really hate her.

All doors were closed when she alighted at the twelfth floor except for one. For a second, she almost panicked thinking that the opened door was hers, only to realize that it was the empty unit beside hers. Boxes are stacked in front of the door and the sound of a man's groans can be heard as she came closer.

She battled with herself if she should help or not. As the next-door neighbor, she knew she should, as a sign of welcome for the new occupant, but she also knew that the feeling in her chest is heavier than those boxes. She scoffed at her dramatics but looked down at herself. Her arms were already crying in protest with her handbag and laptop bag and those boxes looked nowhere near light so she forgot being thoughtful for once and unlocked her door. She was about to go inside when a man's voice startled her.

"Hi. Do you live next door?" The man beamed at her but the smile didn't reach his eyes.

Elaine smiled back, a closed-lip one. "And you must be my new neighbor," she offered her hand which the man accepted. "Elaine."

"Ivan. It's nice to meet you," he let go of her hand and gestured at the boxes. "I'll be done in a minute. You don't have to worry about the noises." He smiled again but Elaine can only see a grimace.

"Don't worry, take your time. I would have helped you but—"

Ivan waved his hand no. "No need. You must be tired from work," he observed, noticing the formal attire and the laptop bag hanging on her shoulders. "Go on ahead. Have a good night."

"You too," she returned in a clip tone and sent a brief smile again before going inside. The bang of the door echoed throughout the dark empty unit, reminding Elaine that she had no company anymore, that she had to spend the night alone in her empty apartment.

A tear escaped down her cheeks, which ended with bouts of sobbing for the third consecutive night.

—-

There are things in life that once you get a taste of, you'd never want to let go. And for Elaine, that was her relationship with Christian.

They started dating a little over a year ago, when they met at a mutual friend's party, though neither are close enough to the celebrant and her friends so they ended up chatting the night away. A week later, they found themselves agreeing to date exclusively.

Elaine did not have high hopes with her relationship at the start. Christian seemed to be the happy-go-lucky type of guy who always acted on a whim instead of having plans. She wasn't in too deep yet, so she didn't mind it at all.

But as the months go by and their relationship turned for the better, people around them started to notice—that Christian is changing for the good and it was mainly because of his relationship with Elaine. It flattered the female, she won't deny it. Knowing that she may be one of the reasons why Christian was trying to find a stable job, having the courage to pursue his passion in photography, and planning for his future, made her pleased.

All along, Elaine was expecting that she was included in the plan. It only dawned on her that she was never part of the picture when one day, she got home, expecting the smell of pepperoni and cheese for their usual pizza night, only to find a large bag filled with all of Christian's things that had accumulated in her home. They never agreed to stay together officially but they might as well be for all the days and weekends the male had stayed with her.

At first, she thought he was going for a vacation. She could've accepted it, a six-month out of the country trips to take images of the wonders of nature. What she didn't understand was why he had to break up with her.

They could've made it worked, Elaine believed so. She trusted herself to stay faithful and she put the same amount of trust on Christian. It just so happened that her ex-boyfriend did not believe in long distance relationships. It even hurt more when he said that he's not even sure if he's even coming back. His career was just starting, he said. It could be his one in a lifetime opportunity, he said. All Elaine could do was cry and beg him to at least try, but he was already decided.

And that was it. The end of a year-long relationship in just a snap.

—

The pastor was going through the sermon part and Elaine pinched her forearm to stay focused. They had to work overtime last night and she barely had a wink of sleep before she raced to be on time to the church.

Attending the mass was a weekly thing for Elaine. Christian never accompanied her no matter how much she forced him to and now, she's secretly grateful because at the least, she has this one activity she was used to doing alone.

The pastor's voice resounded against the walls and she snapped back into attention. Someone, a man perhaps judging by the black slacks and the scent, sat beside her. She almost rolled her eyes for the man's tardiness but bit her lips when she realized that she was no better for drifting off instead of listening.

The pastor droned on and she could hear the sound of the piano and the jingle of the tambourine but it faded as her lids became heavier.

By the time she woke up, people were standing up and were walking towards the exit. Elaine jolted in her seat, lifting her head from a sturdy shoulder she was leaning on, cheeks crimsoning due to the embarrassment.

She looked to her right and her eyes widened while the color of her cheeks got redder. "Ivan," she muttered. Of all people to fall asleep on while a mass was ongoing, it had to be her new next-door neighbor.

Ivan chuckled and raised his hand to his lip, which confused Elaine. When it dawned on her, she turned around and wiped the bit of drool that escaped her lips.

Clearing her throat and checking discreetly if there was still drool left, she turned back again to an amused Ivan. At least now, the smile reached his eyes unlike the first time she saw him.

"I'm sorry for falling asleep on you," she pursed her lips. An old lady passing by gave her a stink eye and she refused to shrink on her seat in shame.

Her neighbor saw the gesture and he chuckled. "It's okay. You went home late didn't you?"

"How did you know?" Her eyebrows furrow.

Ivan looked more amused now. "I heard your door. It wasn't exactly hard to when it's the dead hour of the morning," he explained.

Elaine nodded, laughing at herself for thinking of anomalous things such as Ivan being a stalker or a creep. It crossed her mind that it was still strange for him to be awake at such an hour but then that would mean it was also strange for her to have just come home so she didn't bring it up.

"Oh!" She unconsciously glanced over his shoulder and found a tiny, wet mark. Scrambling for tissues, she pulled a handful and wiped at his clothes furiously. "I am so sorry," she apologized repeatedly until Ivan had to hold her hand to stop her.

"It's spit. No big deal. No one's gonna die," he smiled once again. Elaine thought he should smile more often. It brightens up his face. Meanwhile, her face was on fire.

"Can I treat you for coffee then? As sorry and welcome?"

"I'd love to but I have somewhere to be. Maybe next time," he said noncommittally.

"Next time then." She apologized again before racing back home. A loud 'I'm home' is on the tip of her tongue but she stopped herself just in time.

Elaine dragged her feet to the sofa and flopped down unceremoniously with her legs hanging on an arm. Tears cascaded down her temples, which progressed into sobs. Her chest felt tight and her breath was constricted.

Earlier, she prayed to God to give her Christian back. She wished that Christian would change his mind and call her, or at least send her a message, saying sorry and that he wants her back.

She was praying but the pain hurt like hell. She asked God why did this have to happen to her, why she had to feel such pain, why she had to feel hopeful for her future for once, only for it to crumble right in front of her.

It was so unfair. She gave it her all but all she got was nothing.

—-

It had been a month since the breakup and Elaine was faring better. She haven't cried herself to sleep for two weeks now and she even had the energy to go out for a walk. It wasn't much but it was a start. She still thought of her ex-boyfriend from time to time, which was inevitable considering every corner of her apartment reminded her of him, but the pangs were getting less painful. In a way she didn't know how, she was getting by.

It was a Sunday and she was on her way to the church. A friend, Leslie, welcomed her with a hug.

"You're looking great, dear." The shorter female brushed her cheek against Elaine's and Elaine had to chuckle at her affections.

"Hi, how have you been? I haven't seen you here lately?"

Leslie beamed at her in delight. "I went on a vacation with Luis to France. Oh, we have to get some coffee later. I have lots of stories to tell you," she narrated giddily, the smile never wavering off her face.

"How's Christian? Still sleeping I bet?" Leslie chuckled and Elaine's eyes twitched. She swallowed a lump in her throat and an awkward silence passed before her friend realized that something was wrong.

"Hey, what's wrong?"

Elaine cleared her throat and forced a smile. "W-we broke up," she cursed at herself for stuttering. It felt more real every time she had to say it outloud and it doubled the sharp pain that coursed through her.

Leslie looked shocked beyond belief at the news and scrambled to wrap her arms around Elaine again. "I'm so sorry!"

Elaine, who had to fight the tears that were threatening to come out, hugged her back, glad to have someone to comfort her even if it was a month late. "It's okay. It's been a month."

She pulled back and wiped the tears that escaped despite her resistance. "I'm all right," she forced out a smile. Her friend looked at her worriedly but let it go for now. "All right, let's have lunch together okay?" Leslie asked, to which Elaine said yes. It had been a while since she had a meal with another person aside from her co-workers and she welcomed the thought now more than ever.

The mass lasted for a little over an hour and Leslie pulled her to a nearby Italian cafe that served great pasta and gelato. Elaine was grateful for the distraction but she could not help but glance at a table for two at a corner. She mentally sighed and erased the memories in her head.

—-

Elaine was working on a report when a call came. Not expecting anybody, she looked at her phone quizzically, which registered Leslie's name. Leslie rarely contacted her through the phone.

Surprised, she accepted the call and had to brace herself for a joyful Leslie who almost screeched a 'hello.'

"Hey, what's up?" Elaine reclined back on her seat and shut her eyes. She could hear her stomach grumbling only to remember that she didn't eat anything for lunch.

"I know this might be too soon, but it's been two months and it's not too soon right?" She said rapidly and Elaine had to sit up straight again and focus on her words to keep up.

"What exactly might be too soon?"

Leslie paused dramatically. Elaine could almost hear her excitement through the receiver.

"Dating."

"Dating?" Elaine repeated dumbly.

"Yeah, dating. I figure it's about time you meet new people. What do you think?" Elaine processed everything before saying an alarmed 'what' as a reaction.

She sighed before continuing. "Leslie, I know you have the best intentions in mind. But if you still didn't know, I barely have time to meet new people."

"But you have the time," Leslie insisted. "Every Sundays. Don't you always save your Sundays?"

"I do. But that's for church and some me time. I don't feel like going to a party or anything after a mass."

"Exactly. For church. And forget the me time, you have more than enough of that," Leslie paused and apologized for the insensitive remark, which Elaine only waved away. Leslie was just telling the truth.

"What I actually wanted to say is that I know this guy, from the church we go to, who you might be interested to meet," Leslie drawled on. It took a minute before it registered what she was suggesting.

"Are you setting me up on a blind date?" She asked incredulously.

"Uh, yes," her friend admitted sheepishly.

Elaine rubbed a thumb on a temple. "Do I have a say on this?"

"Not really. I already set up the time and date."

"Leslie—!"

"I had to! I know you're gonna say no!"

"Whatever. Just text me the details. I have work to do," Elaine grumbled. She heard a faint 'I love you' before she hung up the phone and she felt a little bad for not saying it back to her dear friend.

—-

That night, Elaine turned and tossed on her bed. She couldn't stop thinking about the blind date and she had bombarded herself with too much questions that only left her more confused and doubtful.

Is it too soon? What if Christian knows about it? What if the guy isn't what she's expecting him to be? But then, what exactly are her expectations?

The fact that he goes to her church is a good point, but the thought that she saw it as a good point gnaws at her guilt. It might be ridiculous but she felt guilty for indirectly saying yes to the blind date. It had been two months but thinking of a possibility of a relationship with anyone other than Christian brought a bad taste to her mouth.

Elaine pushed the glass door open before a waitress assisted her to her seat. A man was already seated at the table, but she could not see his face yet.

A gasp escaped her lips when the waitress stopped and gestured at their table, making the man look up.

"Elaine?" Ivan said, sounding shell-shocked himself.

"You're Leslie's friend?" Elaine asked for good measure. She had not seen her neighbor for weeks now. The last time, they only exchanged brief hellos when they happened to meet while taking out trash.

Ivan stood up and helped her pull her seat back, before returning to his own side.

"And you are Leslie's friend," Ivan jokingly deadpanned. Elaine took her seat and began to chuckle. Ivan, amused by the situation, also began to laugh.

"I guess we'll be having a date today?" He asked with a smile on his face. Elaine hummed in affirmation while smiling from ear to ear.

"How did you meet Leslie?" Elaine asked once their food was served.

"I actually knew Luis first. He was an old friend and he was the one who suggested this place for me to move to," Ivan explained before taking a bite of the grilled chicken.

Elaine took a sip of water before responding. "Why did you move? Was it for your job?"

The question froze Ivan for a second before he relaxed. Elaine bit her tongue for the question which obviously hit a nerve.

"You don't have to answer it if you don't want to," She said softly.

"Sorry," he offered a timid smile.

"It's okay," she smiled before diverting the conversation to a different topic.

It turned out that they have a lot of similar interests than they could have expected. They have the same fascination with the Harry Potter series, the same geeky side when it came to Star Wars, and the same passion when it came to football—though Elaine loved Man U with a passion while Ivan preferred Chelsea.

Hours later, they found themselves laughing comfortably around each other while they walk together home. They stopped when they reached Elaine's door and Ivan kept a good distance, to which Elaine was grateful for.

"I really had a lot of fun," Ivan smiled.

"Me too. I think it's been ages since I've laughed that much," Elaine gushed.

He put his hands in his pant's back pockets and Elaine mentally chuckled.

"We should do this again some other time?" It was more of a question rather than a statement.

Elaine let out a deep breath she didn't know she had been holding and nodded. "Sure."

—-

She threw the frame inside the black plastic bag and flinched at the sound of breaking glass. Next were the t-shirts and boxers that were definitely not hers, followed by other toilet utilities that were never meant for a woman.

It was a day after her blind date and last night, she had the urge to throw away everything that reminded her of Christian. It had been months but she still kept some of his belongings that he left there, silently holding on to the hope that he would come back.

This move did not mean anything but a sign of her trying to move on. She had been meaning to do it for weeks but the date with Ivan was the last push she needed to start working on it. She sniffed and sobbed for the first few minutes but it got better as the plastic bag got fuller.

It was filled with pictures, letters, dried flowers, candy and chocolate wrappers, and almost every single thing that Christian gave her during their relationship, including the bracelet that he gifted to her last Christmas. It took a lot of emotional effort but afterwards, she felt lighter, as if an invisible baggage was thrown away.

The door next to her opened just as she was pulling the plastic bag outside to throw it in the bin. Ivan looked as surprised as she was. He was sporting a shirt paired with loose shorts and running shoes.

"Going for a run at night?" She asked, eyeing his outfit.

Ivan shrugged. "The park's good enough for some laps."

Elaine stopped for a second to think before taking a leap of faith. "Mind if I join you?"

—

The night was a bit chilly but fortunately, there was minimal wind.

Elaine had been living in that neighborhood for years but it was the first time that she jogged at the park. She always thought it was full of rowdy teenagers getting drunk or creeps who had nothing better to do with their lives. Ivan laughed at her when she voiced it out.

"This place's actually good," He panted, arms swinging as they jogged around the vicinity. "You should just avoid Friday nights because it can be too crowded."

She looked at him curiously. "How long have you been going here?" She asked, breaths coming short. Ivan slowed his pace a bit.

"Since the first week I moved," he answers. "It was a bit lonely staying indoors."

Elaine stopped in her tracks, causing Ivan to stop too.

"I am so sorry for being a very unwelcoming neighbor. I should have made you something and came over to check on you."

Ivan rested a hand on her head and ruffled her hair. Elaine felt like pulling away but didn't, surprised at how large his hand felt. "No need to feel sorry. I know it wasn't your best day then," he continued jogging and she followed automatically.

She gulped as she remembered that day. It was definitely one of her most miserable days. "Yeah. My boyfriend just broke up with me a few days before that," she chuckled dryly. This time, it was Ivan who stopped first.

"I am so sorry to hear that."

She pursed her lips in thought. "It's okay. I've been doing great. It wasn't an excuse to not welcome you," she patted his shoulder, signaling him to continue moving.

It was silent for a few minutes before Ivan spoke up again.

"I just got divorced a few months ago."

Elaine screeched to a halt. "What?" Her eyes widen at her rude reaction. "I mean, when?"

"A few weeks before I moved," Ivan looked down. "My ex-wife and I just got divorced and I realized I can't stay at our home for long so I sold it, and moved here," he gestured at his surroundings with feigned enthusiasm. "And I think I made a great decision."

Elaine took a step closer before wrapping her arms around him. "I am sorry to hear that."

She could feel him shaking his head as he hugged her back. "I guess we're both sorry to hear about each other's heartbreaks?" he joked to lighten the mood. She pushed him back and hit him lightly on the chest before laughing.

They both broke into fits of laughter, earning the questioning looks of the passers-by.

—

They continued to contact each other throughout the week. They may be neighbors but Elaine frequently opted to work until late night so they can't really meet much. Leslie called once to check on how the date went and squealed when Elaine responded with a simple 'Thank you' and shouted 'I knew it, I knew it' repeatedly until it burned Elaine's ears.

The following Sunday, Elaine and Ivan agreed to go to the church together, causing Leslie to get excited upon seeing them.

She looked at them knowingly and winked at Elaine, who blushed at her friend's action. Ivan chuckled at the sight but pretended that he did not see it. All of them, including Luis, Leslie's boyfriend, sat side-by-side inside the church.

During the mass, Elaine prayed and asked for guidance, if what she was doing was right or if it was too soon to consider liking a different man. When she opened her eyes and looked at Ivan's direction, she found him to be staring back at her.

She glanced away and fought down the blush that crept on her cheeks.

—

It was a Wednesday night and usually, Elaine would still be at work, doing things that were not really urgent.

When she got home, it was way too early for bedtime and she found herself thinking of the man living in the unit beside hers. Curiously, she laid an ear flat on the surface of the wall to check for any noises. She didn't know why but she wanted to check if Ivan was home.

She could hear a faint sound of music and she thought about it once, twice, and multiple times before deciding to send him a message.

A few minutes later, there were knocks on her door. Elaine, already clad in more comfortable clothes, welcomed the sight of Ivan carrying chips and soda.

"Did you bring any DVDs?" She helped him bring the things to her living room and settled them on the coffee table. Ivan reached for his back and pulled out some cases and handed them to her.

She raised her eyebrows at the choices. "So you're basically suggesting we watch the whole series of Harry Potter?" She looked at him pointedly.

Ivan shrugged before making himself comfortable on the couch. "Pretty much," he grinned.

In the middle of the movie, they found themselves sitting close to each other, shoulders almost bumping. Elaine looked at her side and it was only a few inches away from Ivan's. Unconsciously, she continued to stare until he looked back.

"Like what you see?" he grinned mischievously, earning a smack on his chest.

"Your scar," she started, pertaining to a small scar at the left corner of his lips.

"Ah, they're battle scars," he jested. Her forehead scrunched at the vague answer.

Ivan sighed before reclining fully. "I had a bit of a scuffle last year. I saw my then wife with another man and I confronted them right on the spot. And the rest is history," he smiled but the bitterness was pronounced.

Elaine copied his position and leaned her head on his shoulder. It was a bold move and she was holding her breath if the male would shrug her off. However, Ivan lifted his arm and rested it on her shoulder so she could scoop closer. Elaine let the tension seep out of her body.

"I only have one question," she said after a while.

"What is it?" He closed his eyes, hoping that he could answer it whatever the question was.

"He got it worse right? I mean, you managed to hit his face at least twice? With bruises?"

Ivan burst out laughing. "Yes, yes, I did. I kicked him in the stomach, too. It was pretty satisfying," he answered, still chuckling at the unexpected question.

"Good," She said before placing an arm over his stomach.

They watched the rest of the movies in the same position.

—-

Elaine was typing her report when her boss approached her.

"I read your latest report, about the success rate if the company decides to venture in e-commerce." She waited with bated breath. It was a report she had been working extra hard for.

"And I can say I'm impressed. I sent a copy to the higher-ups and we just have to wait for their comments," he patted her on the shoulder.

Elaine beamed and said thank you.

"You should continue doing what you've been doing recently," he commented, puzzling Elaine.

"I mean, you look happier. Whatever the reason is, continue doing it," he said before turning back to his office.

Elaine could only think of one big change in her life recently. Biting her lips to stop herself from grinning too widely, she smiled at the thought of a man.

—

She was preparing the TV and the player for their usual movie night when Ivan received a call. His expression dimmed and his jaw locked when he saw who was calling but still answered it, walking towards the kitchen for some privacy.

Elaine, though worried, stayed where she was and fiddled with her own phone. She tried to give Ivan the privacy he needed but was surprised when his voice got louder.

"I don't give a fuck about it. I'm deleting your number. Please don't call me anymore."

She could hear the sound of a phone hitting the floor and she scrambled off the sofa to check on him.

Ivan was staring at the broken device and his chest was heaving deeply. Slowly, she walked towards him and reached for his shoulders. He relaxed at the touch and rubbed a hand on his face.

"I'm sorry you have to hear that," he reached for her hand and pulled her closer to him before hugging her waist.

Elaine put her hand on his hair and carded her fingers through the black strands.

"It was my ex-wife," he explained, making Elaine halt her actions for a moment. She only resumed when Ivan nudged her hand with his head. "She was telling me about her wedding in two weeks, and that I'm invited." He laughed bitterly. "She cheated on me and she had the guts to invite me to her wedding."

Elaine, now shaken, fought the tears that are threatening to spill. She can feel the hurt from Ivan's voice and it was affecting her more than it should.

She remained silent, listening to Ivan's breath until he completely relaxed and his breaths evened out.

The silence was deafening until Elaine had the courage to break it. "Do you still love her?"

It was a yes-no question but Ivan didn't respond for the next two seconds, nor even for the next minutes.

Feeling defeated, Elaine pulled herself from his grasp, ignoring his pleas to make her stay. She collected her things from his living room before walking her way outside and into her own unit. Ivan knocked on her door for a few minutes until she said from the other side.

"Please. Stop it. I need some time alone."

The knocks stopped, and a few seconds later, another door was shut.

—-

Just months ago, it was Christian who was the cause of Elaine's sleepless nights. It was him who was the reason why she cried and continuously asked herself of what's wrong with her and why do people find it so hard to love her. It was him who was the reason why she didn't want to wake up to face another day and tempted her to just laze on her bed, feeling as if all the energy had been sucked out from her.

But now, just a few months later, Ivan had been occupying her mind much more than she expected he would.

He is a good man. He's nice, funny, responsible, smart, and even good-looking—a complete catch if she dared say. When she first saw him, all sweaty and panting from carrying heavy boxes, she just saw him as just another attractive man who happened to be her neighbor and nothing else. Admittedly, she even forgot about him until their embarrassing encounter at the church. That was how it was, but because of one date, it turned into something more.

Elaine found herself genuinely enjoying Ivan's company as they spent more time together. It started from scheduled dates and movie nights until they found themselves into a routine of being together every other day, whether it was to just talk, share about their day, or watch movies.

It was a routine that they easily adapted too—they never forced themselves into it nor did they set fixed days and to-do lists whenever they meet. Day by day, Elaine found herself thinking of her ex-boyfriend less, and whenever she did, it was to smile at the memories they shared and never to wallow in the sadness and the gaping hole he made when he left.

As Ivan made her feel light-hearted, carefree and secured, she found herself forgetting about the heartbreaking nights, about the times when she went back to an empty home, and about the thrown away pictures and gifts. With Ivan, she felt that she could try again, that she could, maybe, fall in love again.

But it seemed that Ivan thought otherwise. She could still see how hurt he was when he talked about his ex-wife inviting him to her wedding. She could remember how tightly clenched his fists were and how much he was trembling in anger. It was a sight she never expected to see from the usually composed man.

When she asked that question she wasn't hoping for an absolute no. They were married and she knew that he must have felt so strongly for her to ask for her hand. But at the least, she was expecting something along the lines of 'I'm doing fine' or 'I'm getting over it' and it would have sufficed, for her at least.

If anything, it made her realize how much she was wearing her heart on her sleeve yet again. She wasn't in love with him, not yet at least, but she knew she was on her way. All along, she thought he felt the same, that he was moving forward and trying to forget his past heartbreak, just like her. Elaine thought that a part of him had thought about her in a romantic way, that she might be someone who he can ideally like, but then again, those were just Elaine's assumptions.

The problem with her, as always, were her hopes and baseless assumptions. These always manage to fuck her emotionally—big time. She just never learned.

—

Ivan tried to contact her in the following days but she was resolved on avoiding him for a few days. She was aware that she was being immature but she deemed herself unprepared.

Every day, she recited every line she could say once they managed to talk. She imagined different scenarios and how she would react to them and what she should say. She admitted, most of her though-of situations were bad. She wasn't too hopeful that they would be returning back to the friendly yet flirty camaraderie they had formed.

Elaine was far from being level-headed. When it came to feelings, she was like an open book. She never tried to hide what she was feeling nor did she ever lie about it. So when one day, while standing on the train, hand clasped tightly on the handrail, and a man stood behind her and asked "Will you be my girlfriend?" she broke down in tears and attracted the attention of other commuters.

Among all the scenarios she imagined in her head, this wasn't how it was supposed to be. He wasn't supposed to show out of nowhere and tell her things she has been wishing to hear for weeks in the middle of a crowded train. She tried to stop her tears but the various emotions overwhelmed her.

Ivan had panicked, wiping away her tears furiously with his fingers and then the sleeves of his sweater. He was expecting her to shriek or push him away or to give him the finger, but this wasn't in his imagined reactions.

When the train stopped at the next station, he gently guided Elaine out and continued hushing her. Her cries were now reduced to sobs and Ivan cursed at himself for making her cry.

Once she was calm, she smacked him hardly on his chest, before saying a garbled "Yes."

For a while, Ivan was confused why she said that but broke into a large grin when he realized the implication.

Overjoyed, he grabbed her face with both hands and kissed her, right in the middle of the station, with some bystanders looking away from the scene. The kiss was chaste yet sweet. Their lips glided smoothly against each other and for a while, Ivan was tempted to press harder, which was futile when Elaine pushed him.

"But," Elaine sniffed and shushed him with a finger on his lips. "Explain."

"Could I take you home first? It's starting to get cold," he gestured at her working clothes—a thin blouse and a pencil skirt—and led them outside and hailed a cab.

There was a deafening silence throughout the ride home and their way up in the elevator, but Ivan never let go of her hand the whole time.

He led them to his unit instead of Elaine's and she was about to protest but he insisted.

He pushed her until she was seated on the sofa and he sat beside her as closely as possible. She squirmed in her seat and he gave her some space, rubbing his neck sheepishly.

He reached for her hand and turned his body towards her.

He started with a deep breath before launching to his long narrative. "That night, when you asked me if I still loved her, I was sure that my answer was no," He brought a hand up when he saw that she was about to interrupt him.

He continued once she silently agrees to keep on listening.

"But at the same time, I can't say it. It sounds more real once you say it out loud doesn't it? Am I making any sense?" He chuckled. Meanwhile, Elaine responded that yes, she understands because she felt the same thing with Christian.

"We were a couple since high school, and then through college. Most people called us the ideal couple and were just waiting for us to get married. It was as if there was no other way out of it but to build our own family. So I did ask for her hand in marriage and she said yes." Ivan heaved a deep breath, composing his next words in his mind.

"But as soon as we started living together, something felt...weird. A year later, I realized how used we are to being together. We were so used to seeing each other, to doing things together that it only seemed natural that we got married. I realized that maybe, we took marriage for granted, and it was a hurried decision merely out of obligation because of the people's expectations."

"We started to drift away from each other then. In the back of my mind, I knew she was thinking the same thing. When I saw her with another man, it hurt me—not because I still love her but because I was at least expecting that we wouldn't reach that point where we would hide secrets behind each other's backs—especially a lover at that."

"I saw red and then I found myself furious. I was angry at her but more at myself for letting us be trapped in that situation. When we decided on the divorce, it was heartbreaking but it felt like a burden

I never knew I had was lifted from me. It felt liberating." He paused, tightening his hold on Elaine's hand. Elaine returned the gesture, egging him to go on.

"I admit. It still hurts. But not because I still love her but more from the fact that I spent so many years thinking I was happy but realized that I wasn't. It was hard coming to terms with that: that I forced myself to think that everything was alright when it wasn't. And then suddenly, she told me the news that she's getting married and practically screaming at me that she's found her happiness. I'm happy for her. We've been together for so long that I can't even bear thinking of hating her. But then I thought of myself and my sorry state of a coward who can't even ask you to be mine and I was enraged because I felt that it was unfair. I thought that I deserve my own happiness too." His voice trembled then and he blinked repeatedly as his eyes began to get misty.

Elaine knelt beside him and pulled his head to her chest, rubbing his back consolingly at the confession.

"I'm sorry if I hurt you. Because all these just came crashing on me and I suddenly couldn't answer. I didn't know where to start. It felt too much." She felt a wetness on her arm and hugged him more tightly. If she could only take a part of the pain he was feeling, she would do it.

"I'm sorry for assuming the worst, and for not giving you a chance to explain." She muttered, kissing a spot in his head to reassure him that she was there, and she won't be leaving anytime soon.

Ivan retreated and pulled her into his lap, resting his forehead against hers. "I'm sorry for giving you the chance to assume the worst, then. If anything, I just really want to say how much I like you and how much you make me happy." He gave her a peck and kept his lips there, feeling the smile forming on his lips.

"I'm really glad I met you. I'd do anything I could so you could forget him completely."

Elaine shook her head no in protest. "No, Ivan. We will work together so we could heal completely. This is no you helping me, nor me helping you. This is us helping each other," she said, gazing into his eyes lovingly.

He smiled a smile that reached his eyes, the one that Elaine absolutely adored, before replying. "I love the sound of that."

END

MY CHRISTIAN COWBOY

JENNIFER ANN RAMSEY

Chapter One: The Meeting

Bill sat on the porch of his mother's small farm home shining his boots. Bill took pride of his things, and these boots had to last him for the whole season. It was hard to keep boots clean in his line of work.

Bill grew up with his mother in a small town in Missouri. She had lived there since Bill was born over twenty-two years ago. His job took him out west, though. He was a bounty hunter. When someone would break the law, he would go after them and pick them up. When he brought the criminal to the sheriff, he would get a reward. The land wasn't very developed, and most criminals decided to hide out west. Bill worked especially hard to get the job done, which helped develop quite the reputation. Bill needed to catch every criminal he could to get paid. After his father died, his mother was left alone. Bill felt the need to support her. Bill's mother, Annie, didn't exactly like her son's career, but she had to admit that he was good at it.

Annie was starting to wear the wisdom and pain of old age. Her hair was more gray than blonde, and she had wrinkles under her eyes. She was usually seen smiling, though, especially when her son was safe and at home with her. She was known around the small town for her feisty attitude, her cooking, and her talent for making clothes.

"Finish up and come get some of this chili, boy," Annie called out to her son.

"I'm almost done, ma!"

"Well, I don't want to hear a word when your chili is cold."

"Is there cornbread?"

"You ungrateful boy, you better get in here and take what you're given before you get nothing!"

Bill put down his polish and boots and headed into the wooden home. The home was small, but it had a comfortable feeling about it. On the table, next to the kitchen, were two bowls of chili (and cornbread).

"This looks great, ma!" Bill said, sitting down on the bench.

"You are not thinking of having supper before washing up, are you?"

"I'm fine, ma! All I did was go out into town today and get shoe polish."

"You will not sit at my table without washing up. Wash your hands and your face."

Bill obeyed. He spent his days chasing dangerous criminals around the country, but he was still afraid of his mother's whippings.

"So, how long are you staying this time?"

Bill always hated this question. She made him feel guilty, but he had to leave to bring money home. "Sheriff Lawrence told me that he has a job for me. I'm planning on heading there in the morning."

"But you just came home yesterday!"

"I know. I gotta get more money when I can, though. You hardly have any flour left. You have no sugar. I'm glad I came home when I did., but the money that I brought home will only last for so long."

"You know I worry about you when you're not here."

"Just keep busy with church and cooking and your dresses. You won't even know I was gone."

"You know I worry."

Bill saved his cornbread for last. He dipped it in the remainder of the chili in his bowl and took a big bite. "I am gonna miss your cornbread."

After dinner, Annie did the dishes and read the Bible before bed while Bill finished polishing his boots and drank some of his moonshine.

The sun woke Bill up the next morning bright and early. Annie was already up doing her daily chores. Bill went out to feed his horse, Bonnie, and get ready for his next job.

"I suppose I'll see you again in another month or so."

"That depends on how long the job takes me, ma."

"Well, I love you. Be good. I packed you some food to take with you."

With that, Bill got ready for his next job. He rode down to the sheriff's station, and he tied Bonnie up before getting inside. Sheriff O'Malley was a beast of a man. His large stature alone helped to keep order in the area. He also had a large gun that helped.

"Well, there's the top bounty hunter in the whole West looking for another bounty I reckon."

"Well, I need to keep my ma in those nice dress that she makes."

"You know, I've been meaning to tell the wife that it's about time for her to get another Sunday dress. Between you and me, hers is starting to look a little ragged."

"I'm surprised you're willing to spend the money."

"Lord knows I don't want to."

"Well, what have you got for me, Sheriff?"

"To be honest, you've been rounding them up pretty good. We don't have too much right now."

"Come on. You know I gotta work."

"Well, there is one thing, but I'm not sure you'll take it. The Thompsons down in Independence were asking for some help with their daughter. Apparently, they haven't seen her in some time. They will be willing to pay you. They have some money."

"I guess if that's what I need to do then that's what I need to do. I'll head that way right now."

Independence was a bit of a distance, but Bill was sure that she could get there before dinner. He rode throughout the day, only to stop for water a couple of times. When he got to Independence, he stopped at the general store to get some whiskey and some candies. He was also able to ask the person behind the counter to tell him how to get to the Thompson home. He learned that Mr. Thompson was the local pastor, and t he house was just up the road about half a mile.

As Bill came up to the gorgeous but modest house with blue shutters and horses in the back, he saw another site that caught his eye: a young woman in a simple skirt, blouse, and boots. Her hair was in a long, messy braid, and she had the most beautiful smile that Bill had ever seen.

Chapter Two: Katy Thompson and Family

"Excuse me, ma'am. Can you tell me if this is the Thompson residence?"

"I sure can. Katy Thompson. Pleasure to meet you. What brings you around? I haven't seen you here before." The girl spoke with elegance and had a flair of sophistication to her demeanor. Her clothes didn't look especially fancy, but it wasn't Sunday. She also smelled of horses and flowers.

"I'm a bounty hunter and Sheriff O'Malley sent me. I understand that you may need some assistance finding someone.

Katy's eyes lit up. "Oh, come this way. My folks will be so happy to see you. They have been worried sick. Here, let your horse in back with the others. She's not too mean, is she? I don't want her scaring my horse."

"Nope. She's a gentle giant. She'll be just fine."

Katy was moving quickly. "I am so happy that you're here!"

Bill followed the beautiful girl into the family home. The house smelled like cherry pie, and Bill was suddenly painfully aware of how hungry he was.

"Mama! Papa! This man here says he wants to help find Lizzie."

The small family gathered into the main room quickly. Bill could feel the hope in the air the way that the family was so excited.

"Please! Come in. What's your name?"

"Do you know where Lizzie is?

"Are you hungry? Can I get you something to eat? Take off your boots. You're our guest."

When they finally stopped talking, Bill sat down and slowly took off his boots. He could feel the eyes on him.

"My name is Bill. I'm a bounty hunter by trade, and my local sheriff said that you were looking for help. I'm his number one bounty hunter, and I have a very good success rate."

"She's not a criminal or anything," Mr. Thompson said quickly. "She's just always been a little wild. She was always a good girl. She would help me at church every Sunday. It wasn't until recently that she started misbehaving."

"What was she doing to misbehave?"

"Well, she started dating a boy. I told her that I disapproved, but she wasn't going to let that stop her. I often wish that I had just let her date him. Maybe she would still be with us if I had," said Mrs. Thompson.

"Don't blame yourself, mama."

"And you guys have no idea where she might have gone?" Bill asked.

"She probably left with her boyfriend to Shadow Creek. The only problem is that it is quite far away in Kansas," said Katy. "Her boyfriend had family there."

"I simply can't abandon my congregation. They need me."

Bill nodded. "Well, I am happy to go travel down there and bring her back for you. That's no problem."

"Oh, thank you! We will pay you. We will pay you everything that we have. We just want our little girl back," said Mrs. Thompson.

"I will only need a couple of supplies and a small advance. When I return with Lizzie, we can complete the payment," said Bill. "I'll leave tomorrow. Now, as the first part of the payment, do you think that I can have some of whatever smells so darn delicious around here?"

"Yes! Yes! Yes! Katy, go whip him up a plate."

"Absolutely, mama."

"We will have to send the sheriff our thanks for sending you to us. You are the answer to our prayers," said Mr. Thompson.

"Well," said Bill," I appreciate it, but don't thank me too much yet. You can thank me when I come back with your daughter. And maybe I can enjoy one of your sermons then."

"Oh, that would be wonderful. You will be my special guest," said Mr. Thompson.

"What happens if she says she doesn't want to come back?" Katy asked putting a plate in front of Bill. "I mean, why would she just leave with some stranger?"

"I can be very convincing," said Bill. "It's my job to take people where they don't want to go. This will not be new for me."

"You're not going to hurt her, are you?" asked Mrs. Thompson.

"I generally don't even have to hurt the fugitives that I bring in. I don't think that a little woman will be too difficult," said Bill. "The boyfriend might catch a beating, though. It depends on what I find."

Mr. Thompson got a serious look on his face. "Now, I can't condone violence, Mr. Bill. Jesus taught us to turn the other cheek, and I have to maintain that sentiment. However, I would not be upset if you didn't bring him back with you."

"And what's so bad about him?" Bill asked.

"He lives an immoral life. He drinks He gambles. He was exciting, but Lizzie doesn't need excitement. She needs to be at home with her family. She needs to be a respectable girl," said Mrs. Thompson. "It's not acceptable for her to be running off like this."

"And how old is Lizzie?" Bill asked.

"Sixteen-years-old. Almost two years under me," said Katy.

"Well, thank you all so much for the meal and the hospitality. I think that I should be heading to sleep as soon as possible. I want to be sure to leave early in the morning."

"Absolutely. You can sleep in Lizzie's bed for the night. It's next to Katy's. Katy will sleep with us in our room tonight. She can show you where your bed is."

Katy showed Bill the small bed in a small room in the house. "It's not much, but it will do," Katy said giving him pillows.

The next morning, Mrs. Thompson had a nice sack of food and other supplies. As he was getting ready to head out, he saw Katy running in from doing her chores.

"Mama! Wait!"

"What is it, child?"

"Mama, I want to go with."

Chapter Three: A Travel Companion

"You can't be serious," Mrs. Thompson said.

"Mama, please. I know she'll come home if I go with," said Katy.

"And who do you suppose is going to do your chores while you're gone?" asked Mrs. Thompson.

"Mama, I haven't gone anywhere in my whole life. Lizzie just ran off. I just want to go with to get her. To see something new," said Katy.

"I'm not having my second daughter run away too," said Mr. Thompson walking out the front door. "I say we let her go. There's only one problem, Katy."

"What's that, pa?"

"The decision isn't really up to us. You'd be a burden on Bill here. Now, that's not really fair to him is it?"

Bill didn't know how to respond. The girl would be a complete burden. She would slow him down, and she would use up his rations. He would have to protect her the whole time, too. "It can get pretty dangerous out there, little lady. I ride fast, too."

"I can ride faster!" she said quickly. "I've been riding these guys since I was young. I am the fastest "rider in town."

"I'll have to spend my time looking after you. I don't want to see you get hurt."

"I've never fallen off my horse before. I can't imagine that anyone would try to hurt us. It's a simple trip down to Kansas and back. And I will be a help. Not a burden."

Bill scoffed. He didn't care how pretty Katy was, he knew that she was going to be a hassle on this trip. He could also see that she wasn't going to let go.

"Get ready quickly. I'll also need more pay, of course."

"Of course," Mr. Thompson said. "Naturally, you will be properly compensated."

Bill nodded and looked over at Katy who was simply giddy. "Well, hurry up!" he said.

"Oh, yes. Of course!" she said running inside. When she came back out, Bill could already tell that Katy had too much stuff with her.

"Are you sure you want to carry all of that on a ride all the way to Kansas?"

"I'll be just fine," Katy said stubbornly as she started loading up her horse.

"Just don't come whining to me when the load is too heavy for you."

"Jeez. I said that I got it, didn't I?"

Bill could start to see exactly how this trip was going to go. As they started riding, though, he was pleasantly surprised at how well she could ride. He stayed behind her to make sure that he could keep an eye on her, and she maintained a decent speed the whole time. She didn't even complain much. Bill was worried that she would need to stop for a break every hour. She went a good six hours before even suggesting stopping for a drink of water. Her face was sweaty, and she was clearly very thirsty- she drank quite a bit. It made Bill giggle internally because he knew that she had gone as far as she possibly could before stopping to show him how tough she was. He decided to make a point to suggest small stops for water more often.

"We're gonna ride until sundown and then set up camp," Bill said. "Eat a small bite now, but we'll eat when we're settled."

"Are we going to find a store?"

"We have food. There's no need for that."

"I thought that we just had some bread and some preserves."

"Hopefully, I can catch a rabbit or something. We can have some meat."

Katy didn't complain. They just went ahead and continued riding for the four hours that they had planned. It was just after sun dark, and they found a quiet area to set up camp off of the road.

"We didn't do so bad for the first day. We'll probably get there in another two or three days," Bill said as he built the fire.

"I really do thank you for bringing me along," Katy said.

"Yeah. Just try to keep up the same pace as today, and you won't be too much of an inconvenience," Bill said.

When the fire was burning, he pulled out a small flask of whiskey from his jacket.

"Are you going to drink on this trip?" Katy said, sounding amazed.

"Ma'am, I am bringing you along on my trip. I would ask you to be so kind as to not tell me what I can and cannot do."

Katy went silent.

"So your sister- is she in love with the guy?" Bill finally said.

"I'm sorry?" she asked.

"The guy that your sister ran off with- is she in love with him?"

"I suppose that she thinks that she is. I don't know about if they're actually in love, though. I hope not. That will make this whole ordeal a hell of a lot harder."

"If they are in love, don't you think that they should stay together?"

"I guess we'll have to talk to her about that when we get to Shadow Creek."

The two then turned silent again for some time. Bill wasn't used to having women with him on his trips, and he was happy that Katy wasn't too chatty. He didn't mind the company, though.

"You know I've never been this far out before. It's absolutely beautiful," Katy said. "It's like seeing the world through different eyes. I'm in a different state doing a different job. You get to travel like this all the time?"

"Yep," said Bill.

"You know, I think they have more stars here than in Independence. Or the stars seem brighter. Something just makes them better here."

"Yep," said Bill. He took another swig out of his flask.

"Does that make you fall over? There was this boy in my school, Johnny. He found his daddy's liquor and started drinking it. He fell over in front of everybody. His daddy beat him so badly that he had to sit on a cushion the next day."

"I can handle my liquor," Bill said.

"Well, I think I'm going to head to bed. I might try to count the stars. Thank you again, Mr. Bill." Katy walked up to him and gave him a big hug. It startled Bill at first, but he went ahead and hugged her back. He didn't know how she did it, but she still smelled like horses and flowers.

"Goodnight."

Chapter Four: Beauty

"Watch where you're going!"Bill called out. Katy was going dangerously fast, laughing the whole time. In fact, she was almost going faster than Bill could manage. She seemed to have a true bond with the horse, and they moved as one. They would lean in the same direction and they both seemed to know when they were going to go for a small jump or go around an object.

"I can go slower if it's too fast for you!" the laughing girl called back.

"It's not too fast for me. I'm supposed to keep you safe. I don't need you falling."

"What? I can't hear you. You're getting pretty far behind, Mr. Bill!"

Bill kicked Bonnie to make her go faster, but the horse was going as fast as she could go. Bill kicked Bonnie again, and she got up on her hind legs, neighing. Bill felt a sharp pain as he fell on the dirt ground. He could see the blood scattered in front of him.

He heard Katy running toward him. Once again, she was laughing. "Seriously, if it was too fast for you, you should have said something. I would have slowed down."

Bill was finally able to get up, but he was still feeling some pain.

"I'm not the one who couldn't go faster. It was Bonnie who couldn't go faster. She's getting old."

"Here, let me help you clean up. Let's go back to that stream we passed."

Bill got back on Bonnie (after apologizing for kicking her) and they gently trotted over to the stream.

"Come here. I have a rag," said Katy. As she stood in front of his with the damp cloth,cleaning his wounds, she was amazingly gentle. When she blew softly on the wound, Bill could see that her eyes were the prettiest color of brown that he had ever seen. She maintained a smile the entire time.

"There. You're all better," Katy said. "You want to sit for a minute?"

"Desperately," Bill said. "I'm also starving."

"Well, we can have these biscuits." Katy handed him some biscuits that she had in a napkin in her pocket.

"Are you eating while riding?"

"I try," Katy laughed. "But mostly I keep them to have them ready for Thunder over there. My mama says I spoil him, but he's always been my favorite."

"You are a very good rider."

"It's my favorite thing in the whole wide world. It makes me feel at one with nature. At one with God. I'd kinda lost that feeling lately, but this trip really helped make me remember how much I love riding Thunder."

"Bonnie's been with me since I was young. It was my first horse, and I took care of her more than I took care of myself. I'd be dirty, but she'd be spotless," Bill said.

"How old is she?"

"She is almost fifteen years old," Bill said. "I'm planning on leaving her with my mom and getting a young stud, but I just can't bare to part with her."

"You'll still see her all of the time," said Katy. "Well, is it time to get back to it? We have a long way to go still."

"Yeah," Bill said. "Let's get going."

They rode at the same pace as the day before and continued through the wilderness. The further they got, the more distracted Katy got by the sites.

"Are those buffalo? Look! I think that there are buffalo down there."

"The town has an entire shop just for ice cream?"

Bill knew that he had to focus on the job at hand, so he kept the mesmerized girl on track. They didn't stop once, although he secretly wanted to show her the sights as much as she wanted to see them. He never wanted to do that before. Could this girl be having an effect on him?

They continued traveling until sundown. Their routine was very similar to their routine the night before. They set up camp off of the road, Bill created a fire, and they had dinner by the fire. Bill noticed that Katy was a little closer to him than she was the night before.

"Tell me about yourself, Bill."

"What's there to tell? I grew up in St. Louis. My dad was gone when I was little. I work to help take care of my ma and my horses."

"Do you have a wife?"

"Nope."

"Do you ever want a wife?"

"I never thought about it before."

"Have you ever kissed a woman?"

"Plenty of times."

"You scoundrel!"

"Not at all. It just never works out."

"Do you like your job?"

"Yep."

"Are you ever lonely?"

"Not really. No."

"Do you think that I'm pretty?"

"Yep. You look fine."

They both went back to eating until they finished their dinner. Katy immediately got up to clean the supplies before bed. Bill sat back and sipped on his whiskey until she came back.

"'The stars are amazing again tonight."

"I reckon they are."

"How many stars do you think there are?"

"Millions. Maybe more."

"I'm just going to lay here and watch the stars."

"That sounds nice."

Katy laid down on the ground next to Bill. She gently laid her head against his shoulder. They sat in silence, and she stared at the stars. Bill hoped that she couldn't feel his heart beating a little more quickly than normal while she was so close. They laid there together for a good twenty minutes.

"I think I'm going to head to bed now," Katy said. And she got up and kissed Bill softly. Bill was shocked but received her kiss tenderly. Her lips were the softest that he had ever felt. "Goodnight."

Chapter Five: A Gift

"Let's get going!" called out Bill. "If we hurry up, we will be able to get there tonight."

"You really think so?" asked Katy.

"It's a stretch but maybe. If not, we'll be very close. We can get there early tomorrow."

"This wasn't so bad!"

"This wasn't that far of a ride. Trust me, it can be quite grueling."

"I believe you! I am starting to feel it in my legs."

They continued to ride through the countryside together only stopping for water and short breaks. Bill started to get excited for even those short times with the beautiful girl. She was pretty, she was funny, and she was tough. Most importantly, he hadn't felt quite so alive as he did on this trip with her. He felt privileged to even be able to drink water next to her. He wasn't sure how to interpret the kiss from the night before. They had not talked about the kiss at all, and it was the only thing that Bill could think about.

It was still light when they got to a small town.

"Hey, let's stop here for awhile," Bill said.

"Can we get some candy maybe?" asked Katy.

"We might be able to do that."

They tied up their horses and started walking around the small town. People were outside, and it was a gorgeous night out. Katy's hair was in her usual long braid that always had some wild strands framing her face.

"So were you just tired?" Katy asked.

"Naw. I saw this little town and thought we might enjoy some civilization."

"Well, you have me with you!"

"And you're wonderful company. I also wouldn't mind some candy, though."

"Look! There's the general store. I'm sure my folks will give you an extra couple of dollars for anything you buy me on the trip."

"I'm not worried about it," Bill said.

The general store was larger than most small town general stores. It had a large selection of everything from food, cigarettes, tools, animal feed, crafts, Bibles, clothing, and jewelry.

"Look at that Bible! It's absolutely beautiful!" said Katy. She ran to an ornate Bible with bold colors and fantastic pictures. Katy flipped through the Bible excitedly. This is the most beautiful thing that I had ever seen!"

"It's quite stunning."

"I wonder how much it is."

"More than we have," Bill said. "It sure is nice, though. They have a lot of nice things at this store."

"I know! Look at that bracelet. That looks like real silver. Do you think that there's real silver in there?"

"I think so. And it looks like there is turquoise, too."

"It's the most beautiful thing that I had ever seen. Oh, the other girls in town would be so jealous if they saw me wearing this. This is better than most wedding rings."

"Let's get back to the candy."

Bill and Katy looked through the numerous cartons of candies and picked out a couple of bags full to take with them. Bill also went ahead and bought a coca cola for them to share outside before riding more.

"Well, we should probably get headed out," Bill said.

"Yep. I'm glad that you suggested stopping here, though."

"Go get the horses ready and I'll be right there, OK?"

"Yes, sir."

Bill waited until Katy was out of view before going into the store to buy the silver bracelet and the Bible.

They rode on until they couldn't see anymore and set up camp.

"Are we close?" asked Katy.

"We'll make it by tomorrow."

"Great. I'm so excited to see my sister."

"She'll be happy to see you, too. I think it will definitely help in getting her to come home."

"I hope that she's not with that good for nothing man of hers anymore."

"Did you save her any pieces of candy?" Bill asked.

Katy had her last piece of candy in her hand and threw it into her mouth and shrugged. "I came all the way out here to come get her. Not bring her candy."

After they had a small dinner, Katy took care of their supplies again. She was very good at keeping things clean. When she got back, she immediately sat very close to Bill and put his arm around her.

"I like watching the stars with you," Bill said.

Katy shushed him and continued looking up into the sky. While she sat with his arm around her, she linked fingers with him. Bill loved the feel of her soft, small fingers in between his.

After a couple of minutes, Bill took her face in his hands and brought her in for their second kiss. She leaned in for more, but Bill leaned back.

"I got you something," he said .

"You have more candy?"

"I think you might like it a little more than that." Bill went into his pocket and pulled out the silver and turquoise bracelet that Katy had loved so much in the store.

Katy's eyes lit up. "It can't be! Bill, I- I love it. Oh, but we have to take it back. My parents will never let me have it. It costs too much. They can't pay you back."

"No. This is from me. I want you to have it."

"Are you sure?"

"I'm very sure."

Katy started to tear up, and she immediately took the bracelet and put it on. "It's the most beautiful thing in the whole wide world!" she screamed. She then wrapped her arms around Bill's neck and passionately kissed him.

"You can't wear it while you're riding," Bill said.

"I know."

"It's for church and when you have company over and all."

"OK"

"And you have to clean it once a month."

"Oh, please just kiss me."

Chapter Six: Lizzie Thompson

The sun lit Katy up like an angel. Bill had woken up early to get to Shadow Creek as soon as possible, and Katy was still sleeping in her blankets.

"Good morning!"

Katy woke up in a bit of a daze.

"It's not even light out yet."

"We're getting an early start. We don't want to get to your sister any later than we have to."

Katy and Bill were on the trail before anyone else that morning. They traveled with purpose, and they traveled quickly.

"How long do you think that it will take us?" Katy asked.

"It will probably be about four hours. Maybe six. I'm hoping that we get there by noon."

At their first stop to let the horses drink water, Bill couldn't help but cuddle with Katy on the river bank.

They continued riding throughout the morning enjoying the breeze hitting their face and continually exchanged jokes throughout the ride. They even raced a little bit across one clear meadow.

"We're coming up to Shadow Creek!" Bill screamed.

"We are?"

"Yep! We'll be with your sister soon enough!"

Bill was right- they rode up to the town shortly after. It was another small town. It wouldn't be too hard to find Lizzie.

"Can I put my bracelet on while we're in town?"

"Don't be silly. It's for Sunday and special occasions. You'll wear it to church the next time you go."

"Well, I'm showing Lizzie. Now, how do we find her?"

"Let's start by asking at the general store. Everybody in town has to shop there."

The couple went into the store and Katy immediately started running.

"Lizzie!" she screamed. Lizzie was there at the general store. It was the perfect timing.

Bill watched the two girls embrace before introducing him.

"Hi, Lizzie. I'm Bill. I came down here with Katy to get you."

"I'll tell you everything after I'm done scolding her for running off in the first place. What were you thinking? What about ma and pa?"

"I'm so sorry, Katy. And I'm so glad that you're here. He's awful. He's absolutely awful."

"What did he do to you, Lizzie? Does he beat you?"

"Once. He drinks and yells a lot, though. I made a horrible mistake. I need to go home."

"Well, mama and papa are going to be happy to have you back. But we gotta go tell him that you're leaving."

"He's gone for the day. I don't want to wait to tell him. I just want to take the horse and go now. I'll leave a note."

Bill, Katy, and Lizzie went back to Lizzie's small home to leave a note for the man that she was leaving. Bill didn't want to get too involved, but he was secretly very happy that he could bring Lizzie back to her family and away from the abusive boyfriend. He was also just happy to see how relieved Katy was.

It didn't take long for the three to start to head back to Independence. The girls spent a good portion of the first day of the trip talking in secret. Bill could only assume that it was girl talk about him. When they set up camp for the night, he immediately put his arm around Katy in front of her sister.

Lizzie started teasing them and asked desperately to see the bracelet that Katy had been going on about. He brought out the bracelet and started realizing that he could truly enjoy a life with Katy. There was only one very important thing to do first.

They made it back in four days. The sun was going down, but no one wanted to camp another night. They pushed through until they finally saw the small gorgeous house with the blue shutters. Bill followed the girls as they excitedly put their horses away and got ready to surprise their parents.

Mr and Mrs. Thompson were in the main room by the fire when they walked in. They had huge smiles and both ran to Lizzie to greet her.

"Oh, honey. Why would you do that to us? I'm so glad that you're home," said Mrs. Thompson, hugging her daughter.

"Lizzie, you have a lot of chores to make up," Mr. Thompson said.

"Let her relax at least for the night," said Mrs. Thompson. "You put your stuff away and clean up and relax tonight. You are going to be worked pretty hard in the morning, though."

"I can't thank you enough for bringing our daughter back home to us," Mr. Thompson told Bill.

"It was truly my pleasure, sir. Your daughters are both amazing people. In fact, Katy and I got really close on the trip-"

"Daddy! Bill bought Katy the prettiest ring I've ever seen! And she said that they kissed!" Lizzie blurted.

Mr. Thompson gave Katy and Bill a suspicious look for a moment. "I assume that you are a good person if you were sent here by Sheriff O'Malley. I look forward to getting to know you while you court my daughter."

Katy looked relieved. "Oh, thank you, daddy. Thank you! Let me show you the bracelet."

"Thank you very much, sir. I really was hoping for your approval. I also got a small present for you as well. I know that you're a man of God, so I thought that it would be a nice addition for either the home or the church," said Bill.

"What are you talking about?" Katy asked.

"I didn't tell you, but I got your dad a gift, too. I wanted to ask for the right to court you properly. I'll be right back."

Bill came back with the elaborate Bible that he and Katy had seen at the General Store. The whole family was in awe, and everyone passed the beautiful book around.

"This will be the nicest Bible at the church," Mr. Thompson said.

"Come on, sweetheart," Katy said. "Let's go look at the stars."

THE WINDOW BETWEEN US

CORA LAYNE

Chapter One

Loss

"I'm sorry, Claire. I just can't carry you anymore. I've made excuse after excuse to the school district in your defense. I'm sorry, but we have to let you go," Principal Hayes told Claire with a pained expression.

"Principal Hayes, how could you fire me at this point in my life?" Claire exclaimed tearfully, "My career is all I have left. I can do better, you know that."

"Claire, I'm going to tell you this as a friend—take this time to heal and get yourself back together. You are not the same since your divorce. I understand that this is a very difficult time for you. However, the students need the old Claire, not this Claire; you're constantly late, you've completely neglected the lesson plans required by the district and parents have reported about the inappropriate remarks you've made in the classroom. You didn't even show up to your own classroom's parent-conference day, for goodness sakes!"

"Do you want me to lie to them? Do you want me to tell them that life is all about rainbows and fairy tale endings?" Claire asked angrily.

"See, that is the kind of behavior that the district and I are concerned about. You are no longer fit to be in charge of these students and I will not tarnish my reputation with the school board for you! Please, you need help; focus on yourself right now, Claire. Give yourself a break. Your career will always be here but you are no good if you're behaving like a deranged woman!"

"You can't fire me for getting divorced! Where is your compassion? I've been a loyal employee of this district for ten years! You mean to tell me that nobody in this entire district has gone through what I'm going through?" Claire cried.

"You're clearly missing the point, my dear. You are being fired because your personal life has affected your performance as a teacher in this school and you are putting your students in jeopardy. Please, try to understand and be professional about this. If you'll excuse me, I have an appointment with a parent coming up shortly," he said coldly as he sat in his cushiony, leather office chair.

Claire knew he was not trying to be rude to her, after all, he'd always been kind to her in her years of employment there. While she knew that the principal had no ill intentions for firing her, she still felt betrayed. There was no point in fighting to keep her job; it was obvious that the decision had already been made and set in stone. She slowly got up from the chair across the principal's desk and said, "Well, I guess that's it then. I will have all of my belongings cleared out of my class by the end of the school day. Thank you for everything, Principal Hayes." He gave her a sad half-smile and held out his hand expecting a handshake, but Claire had already started towards the door.

On her way home, Claire thought about Principal Hayes' words about her. He was right, she was not the same. I could never be that Claire again. That Claire thought that Tim would always love her regardless of being infertile. She was naive and she was wrong because in the end—he left her. Claire had once heard from a psychologist friend of hers that when a person goes through a divorce, they go into mourning. Indeed, they do not experience the physical death of their spouse or their loved one, but they do experience the death of a future they dreamed of, worked for, and built along with their partner. Now, she felt like she had no future. She hadn't ever planned on being without him.

As she was driving, it occurred to her to pass by the drive-through of their favorite burger place. Every Tuesday, she would pick him up late after work and they'd eat in the car. They'd always share an order of French fries. So, she ordered herself a cheeseburger and an order of fries. She parked herself on the lot and ate her burger first. When she got to eating the French fries, she ate a couple then looked at the cardboard tray for a moment. She slowly returned the fry she had held up to her lips. It's too big to finish it all by myself. Claire began to sob uncontrollably. What little hope she felt. The one thing she had left had been snatched from her, too. Images flashed through her mind of future Tuesday's sitting in the car in this very lot, crying pathetically over her loss. Truly, it was impossible to imagine herself doing something else.

In the midst of her misery and self-pitying, her cell phone rang. She thought about letting it go straight to voice-mail but it was her father who was calling. Claire's father rarely called unless it was urgent, therefore, she wiped her face and composed herself.

"Hello. Dad?" she answered into the phone.

"Hello, Claire. Are you at work?" her father asked.

"No, I'm not. The last time you called me, it was to tell me that Ginger had swallowed a ping pong ball! I'm kind of worried about what it is this time," Claire chuckled.

"It's not about Ginger this time," her father replied before going completely quiet.

"Huh? Who is it about? Dad, are you okay? How's mom?" Claire was beginning to feel the dread creeping into her. She could hear her father taking deep breaths as if not to burst into tears.

"Dad, what is this about?"

"Your mother," he said, his voice breaking.

"What happened to my mom?" Claire asked desperately, "Has something happened to her?" Her eyes began to water as the worst possibilities started playing in her mind.

"Last night—your mother suffered a stroke. Today, the doctor has told me that your mother suffered some brain damage that might result in permanent paralysis. We won't know the exact extent of her brain damage until they can observe her while conscious. I'm afraid your mother is in a coma at this moment, Claire," her father managed to tell her in a trembling voice.

"Why didn't you call me as soon as it happened?" Claire asked sternly.

"I wanted to wait for the doctor's results. I didn't want to burden you if we didn't have to; I know that's what your mother would have told me. What, with all of what has happened in your life recently, I hesitated."

"I understand but that is my mother. I could be in a coma myself and I'd still want to know how she is!"

"I think it's time we close down our bakery, Claire," her father said sadly, "I'm going to have to take care of your mother full-time. There's no way I would pay for a caretaker to do it for me. I signed up for sickness and in health—taking care of her is my responsibility in these times." Claire got a knot in her throat as she listened to her father speak. I can't even find someone to love me the way my dad loves my mom.

"Dad, that's the only thing paying for your bills right now. What are you and mom going to live off of?"

"We will figure it out. We can move to a smaller apartment in a cheaper part of France or sell all of our belongings." Claire analyzed her situation during the conversation with her father and decided that it would be best if she moved back home to help with the family bakery. She realized right now would not be the best time to close down their only source of income given the circumstances. Her mother was going to need medical equipment, medications, and who knew what else. She wanted to help her parents the only way she knew.

"Let me come home to work at the family bakery," Claire proposed to her father.

"What about your job?" he asked concerned. She thought it best not to tell him that she had been fired to avoid causing more worries.

"I'll ask for a leave of absence or something. Don't worry, Dad, I can take the time off. It's really not a burden. I have to be near mom. You take care of mom and I'll run the bakery until she gets better."

Her father thanked her repeatedly for what she was willing to do to help her family. She had decided to leave the United States to fly across the world, back to her family's home in France. Claire started packing her belongings as soon as she got back to her apartment that night and she booked her flight for the following afternoon. The scare from the possibility of almost losing her mother made her forget about being fired. Claire's world was in shambles but she thought it'd be better if she actually helped her parents than cry pathetically in her car over too many fries. She had no suspicion that she was about to discover happiness in the very bakery where she grew up.

Chapter 2

Danish

Claire arrived in Colmar, France at nighttime. Her mother was in a different part of France in a larger hospital so she made a stop there first. Her father already had her keys to the house and bakery ready for her, as well as a list of duties to be fulfilled at the bakery. She had decided to hire a helping hand at the bakery that she would be paying out of her own pocket. Her father refused to take any money from her but she was persistent and finally convinced him.

"But they won't know the ways of our bakery," her father insisted.

"We will teach them. Dad, you forget I grew up in that bakery. I know it and love it as much as you do. Besides, without you there I am going to have my hands full. I'll make sure to let them know that it is only a temporary job until you and mom can get back," Claire argued.

"I guess you are right. It's just hard to trust someone else with our business. You know it has only been your mother and I working that bakery all these years."

"I know, Dad. But you trust me, right? It will be in good hands. You focus on mom and let me know if you guys need anything." She said her goodbyes to her father and to her mother, who was still unconscious and drove her rented car back to her parent's home.

When she entered her parents' home, she went straight to sleep as she was only getting a couple of hours of sleep before heading to the bakery in the morning to reopen. Claire felt a certain peace being in her parents' home in Colmar, thousands of miles away from Florida. It was almost like being able to relive her childhood and teenage years. She had left to America, met her ex-husband or been married. This is a good place to forget. Her former bedroom was long gone since her parents had it turned into a mini-library of sorts. She put her luggage down in the living room and slept on the couch.

The next morning, Claire woke before the sun rose. She quickly got herself ready and made her way to the bakery which was only down the street—less than a minute's walk. From outside of the bakery, she could see through the windows. The bakery appeared dark and empty. It looked more run-down than it did the last time she came to visit about 5 years ago. Once inside the bakery, she turned on the lights. She went to the back and turned on all of the equipment. It had been a while since she baked anything but, making pastries and sweets had been instilled in her since she was a child. She quickly began to mix her doughs and batters for all kinds of pastries and breakfast bread. The moment she started garnishing the pastries, it dawned on her that she was still quite skilled. The techniques came to her naturally.

A knock at the glass door startled her from her concentration. A glance at the round wall clock in the kitchen revealed that she had gone past 6 o'clock in the morning, which happened to be opening time for the bakery. She ran to the front of the store and looked out the door. It was a tall, light-skinned man with curly hair. His thin, dark glasses framed his hazel eyes. He wore blue jeans with an olive shirt and white sneakers. He waved and a smile revealed the slightest gap-tooth. Claire smiled back at him and quickly opened the door to let him in.

"Good morning," the man said, "am I rushing you? You didn't have to open because of me." Claire recognized his English accent.

"No, not at all. I was just in the kitchen baking," she replied.

"Well, this is a bakery," he laughed. Claire tried to go along with it but she was exhausted from the trip and from baking more than she'd done in ages.

She smiled and said, "What can I get for you today?" The man noticing her disinterest stopped smiling.

"I'll just have a blueberry Danish, please."

"Okay, I believe those are just cooling off on the kitchen rack. I'll be right back with your Danish," she told him politely. When she returned, the man smiled at her again.

"Thank you," he told her as he paid. As he was paying, he also pulled out a little card from his wallet and handed it to Claire. It was a miniature painting he had painted on the card. It appeared to be abstract flowers in a sunny field.

"What's this?" Claire asked holding up the card.

"It's a sunny field to brighten up your day," he said walking out the door.

Claire held the card in her hand and looked at it in puzzlement. At the same time, she was intrigued by the little thing. For the painting being on such a small surface as the canvas, it was extremely detailed. Claire was actually impressed. She taped the card to the wall behind the counter so that other customers could see the man's art. I hope I didn't come off as rude. Claire felt a tad bit guilty from the way she spoke to him. I hope he comes back so I can apologize. She got back to work; still thinking about the man she had been short with. Eventually, she forgot all about it when people started to enter the bakery for their baked goods. Closing time came around so, she cleaned the kitchen and all of the equipment. She was just finished sweeping and about to lock the front door when a young girl walked in. The girl couldn't have been older than 16 years old.

"Hello," the girl said faintly.

"Hi," Claire replied, "what can I get for you?"

"Actually," the young girl said, "I wanted to come in here to ask if there was any help wanted. I could really use the money."

"Why don't you ask your parents for an allowance? You shouldn't have to work. You should be focusing in school."

"That's the thing," the girl replied, "my father abandoned my mother and I not long ago. My mom works but we are struggling to make ends meet. We can't afford to buy my school books. I'm afraid my grades have already begun to suffer." Claire was overwhelmed with compassion for this young girl.

"What is your name?" Claire asked her.

"I'm sorry. I should have introduced myself first— I'm Alice."

"Okay, Alice. I'm Claire, by the way. I'm going to help you out. You have to be here every evening after school. You will help me prep for the next day and we will clean the equipment together. We receive shipments on Sunday mornings and you'll have to be her to help with those, too." Alice immediately began jumping up and down.

"Thank you," she exclaimed repeatedly, "thank you. When do I start?"

"Tomorrow is your first official day," Claire said as she walked behind the counter.

"You can count on me to be here," Alice said excitedly.

"Wait," Claire called out, "take this." She held out a substantial amount of money.

"Oh, I can't take that. That's too much," Alice told her pushing her hand back.

"Sweetie, consider it a hiring or sign-up bonus. Please, take it. I want you to buy your books tomorrow and anything else you might need to do well in school. I can trust you, right?"

"Yes, yes you can. I promise I will buy my books first thing in the morning. How can I ever repay you?"

"You're working for me now, aren't ya?"

"I sure am! Thank you, Miss Claire!"

"Go on home," Claire instructed her, "before your mother starts to worry."

"You got it, Miss Claire. Good night" Alice said as she closed the door leaving Claire alone in the bakery again. Claire finished her cleaning duties and closing routine before heading off to visit her mother in the hospital. As she was exiting the building, she looked at the painting behind the counter and smiled. She was so flustered that morning that she hadn't realized how handsome he was. What goofy gap-toothed smile. Without realizing it earlier, that man had made her entire day. Although, helping Alice made her day as well. The teacher in her would not allow her to not help a student in need of assistance. I failed my students back in America. The least I could do is help a child here at home. Claire recognized that she had been failing at being a role model and a loyal teacher in her last months at the school. It warmed her heart to realize that she still cared for students as a teacher does, whether it is a student from her classroom or not.

Chapter 3

Paintings

Over the next few weeks, the man became a regular customer at the bakery. Every morning, he was there at 6 o'clock ordering a blueberry Danish. Claire still had yet to ask for his name. He hadn't asked for her name so she was unsure about asking for his. One thing he never failed to do, however, was give Claire a new card with a painting for the wall behind the counter every time that he paid. Claire had begun to spend more time polishing herself in the morning EMDASH making sure that she looked out together. One morning the man even complimented her. She started to realize that the man would compliment her every time she wore a new piece of jewelry or had styled her hair differently. Claire decided that she was going to ask for his name the next time he came to the bakery. The thought made her nervous but she thought it was harmless. It's not like I'm asking him to date me. Even though, recently she had begun to imagine herself on dates with this man. I'm going to do it. I'm going to ask for his name.

The next morning, Claire had the man's blueberry Danish all ready for him to take. She placed it in the glass case besides the counter and waited for him to arrive. Alice was there on that particular weekday since it was a holiday and she had no school. She wanted to see what the bakery was like during her school hours. Alice took notice of Claire's appearance that particular day and was curious.

"You're looking dolled up today, Miss Claire," Alice complimented.

"Thank you, Alice. I had a couple of extra minutes this morning and decided to make myself more welcoming or pleasant looking," Claire said fixing her fringe that fell just above her eyes. The rest of her brunette hair was pulled into a high ponytail. Claire had also curled her eyelashes and applied a light pink blush to her ivory skin along with a mauve colored lipstick on her lips.

"That looks like more than a few extra minutes of polishing. Does Miss Claire have a crush?" Alice teased her à la high school mode.

"Are you finished decorating, silly girl? Get back to work," Claire said sternly. Alice made her way to the kitchen and Claire continued to wait. As always, the man arrived at the same hour, same minute as every other day.

"Good morning," he said to Claire as he walked to the counter.

"Hi," Claire replied, "how's your morning?"

"It's always a great morning for me," he said with a smile.

"I have your blueberry Danish ready for you here," Claire said as she took it out of the glass case.

"Wow, thank you."

He started taking out his wallet to pay for the pastry when Claire muttered, "So, I was wondering if—if you'd like to have breakfast with me here." She motioned towards a small café style table set at the corner of the bakery. The man stared at her unbelievingly. There was an awkward silence in the air and Claire had begun to worry.

The man flashed a smile and said, "Uh, I'm sorry I don't think I can. It's not a good time for me." Claire felt the sting of rejection.

"I'm sorry. I shouldn't have asked. Can we forget I asked? Okay, let me just package up your Danish," Claire said clearly hurt.

"Wait, I don't think you understood me," the man began, "I would definitely love to join you very much."

"Oh?" The man took out his wallet and paid for the pastry. He had a small painting for Claire, per usual, but instead of handing it to her, he placed it upside down and wrote something in the back of the card.

"I'm having an exhibit tonight. I'd love it if you'd come," he said as he finally handed the card to her. She looked behind the painting and his writing read: GALLAGHER'S GALERIE. 5 O'CLOCK. His name was also written on the card.

"Okay, I will see you at five—Abe. I'm Claire," Claire smiled.

Abe smiled on his way out the door. Alice appeared from the kitchen and said, "Ooh, Miss Claire's boyfriend is a cutie pie. Get it? Cutie pie. You know, because we work in a bakery."

Claire laughed, "He's not my boyfriend and I doubt he thinks of me that way."

"Well, I'm sorry I spied on you two for a little but I really think he likes you. He was giving you google-eyes as you counted his change and packed his Danish. You should have seen him."

"Did he really?" Claire asked hopefully.

"Uh-huh. What did he write on his painting?"

"It's the name of a gallery a few blocks from here. I'm pretty sure that he's an artist. He invited me to his exhibit tonight."

"Are you going?" Alice asked.

"I don't think I can. I'm usually not finished closing up by that time and I don't want to keep you here that late. It's too risky for you."

"Well, how about we clean up earlier than usual? I think you should give it a shot, Miss Claire. I think he really likes you."

"Alice, you're a child."

"And you are scared," Alice teased. After much persuasion, Alice convinced Claire to attend Abe's exhibit after work. Alice did extra chores in order for them to be able to close the store at four on the dot.

After the store had closed and Alice's mother had picked her up, Claire walked back to her parent's home to get dressed and touch-up her makeup. The thought of Abe gave her butterflies. She had not been on a date with a man, other than her ex-husband, for many years. She was hopeful, yet the dark cloud that had been hovering over her head since her ex-husband left would rain miserable thoughts on her. What if it's all great in the beginning until he finds out? What if he wants children? Claire felt so many fears holding her back. At one point, she even considered pretending to lose the card and not attending. She thought about her previously failed marriage and all the pain it had caused her. The pain she felt when she learned that her infertility was a deal-breaker for the man who had promised to love her in sickness and in health. What if he doesn't want kids, though? I should just be honest. Worst case scenario is he doesn't try to pursue a romance with me.

In the end, Claire decided to visit the exhibit. After all, Abe had always been friendly with her. She tried telling herself that she was only showing support to a good friend. Claire only took a few minutes to arrive at the gallery. There were a few people standing outside looking at the art pieces displayed near the windows. Claire peeked in and immediately concluded that the paintings inside the art gallery were the same style as the miniature paintings Abe had given to add to the bakery's collection. She made her way inside and soon after, Abe found her.

"Claire! I'm so glad you could make it," Abe said giving her a hug. He was dressed to impress in a gray suit and black tie. Claire had not ever seen him dressed so stylish until that point.

"Is this your gallery? I'm seriously impressed. I can't believe I never put two and two together. Of course, you're an artist," Claire said feeling dumb for missing that detail about him. He smiled at her, showing off his gap-tooth and she started to feel that nervousness again. She began to feel the fear of being hopeful and being let down in the end.

"It sure is. I had actually planned to invite you a few weeks back but you appeared to be extremely busy. I didn't want to bother you," Abe told her.

"I see. You were right! I'm only barely starting to get into a routine at the bakery. It's not easy running a business. I hope I didn't appear too unwelcoming but I apologize if I did."

"Oh, not at all. I understand; I was the same way when I first opened up this gallery a couple of months ago. You weren't unwelcoming at all. Truthfully, I was also scouting the place," Abe said.

"Scouting the place?" Claire asked suspiciously,

"Yes. I wanted to make sure your husband or boyfriend wouldn't appear out of somewhere and I'd get a beating for making a pass at a taken woman," Abe laughed. The words rung in Claire's ears.

"Why didn't you simply ask if I was taken?"

"I've kind of always been the shy guy. I spend a lot of time working on my art so I rarely get a chance to ask women out. I'm usually okay with that. But I have a feeling I would have regretted not asking you out," Abe said looking into her eyes. Claire thought that after her divorce it would be hard to ever trust the words coming out of a man's mouth but Abe spoke with such sincerity.

"Well, you finally asked me out," Claire said patting him on the shoulder. The two walked around the gallery talking about his paintings. Abe sounded like a true artist revealing what his inspirations were for each painting. They finally reached the main display. Claire's eyes grew wide and she drew in a gasp. It was a detailed painting of her father's bakery. Abe had painted every wrinkle on the wall, every chip in the paint, every miniscule detail of the bakery was in that painting.

"That's my parent's bakery," she said tearfully.

"Do you like it?" Abe asked.

"Do I like it? I love it. How were you able to capture the details so well?"

"I took a picture of it the day you opened late. Remember? That was the first time we met."

"I do remember. I felt so rude after you had left. I didn't think you'd come back," Claire told him shamefully.

"And I didn't know that I would be tempted to see your beautiful face every day."

"So, are you fairly new in Colmar?"

"I am. I'd only just arrived here the week prior to visiting your bakery. I've been working on a few of these paintings so I haven't had much time to explore." Claire took the chance to invite him on a tour of the city.

"Colmar is a beautiful place. I'm sure you don't need a tour to tell you that but would you like a tour of the city, anyways?"

"Are you asking me on a date?" Abe teased.

"I—," Claire blushed. This was an unusual experience for her. She was not accustomed to pursuing men, especially after her divorce.

"I'm just teasing you, Claire. I'd be honored to have you as my city tour guide," he grabbed her hand and he gave it a soft kiss. The rest of the evening was followed by Abe introducing his favorite baker, Claire, of course, to his friends that had come to visit from England. All of Abe's friends had wonderful stories to tell about him. It was obvious to Claire that he was very loved by many people. His demeanor and the way he carried himself was that of a true gentle spirit. He greeted everybody with a smile and took critique of his artwork with grace but did not allow the praises to inflate his ego. After going home that night, Claire went to bed with a smile on her face.

Chapter 4

Canals

On the Sunday that they had set for their tour of the city, Claire woke up early to meet Alice at the bakery for shipment. She was a little hesitant to leave Alice alone in her father's bakery but she had grown to trust the teenager for her displayed maturity and unfailing responsibility. She made sure to leave the glass cases full of baked goods for Alice and had also prepared a small gift for Abe, which she wrapped in a beautiful decorated box.

As Claire left the bakery she said, "I'm going to call you every once in a while to check on you but please call my cell if you need anything."

"Yes, ma'am! Don't worry, Miss Claire. I've got this under control. Have fun on your date with the painter!"

Claire and Abe had agreed to meet in front of his gallery a few blocks away. It was a few hours until lunch time so they had much time to explore. Claire stood in the front of the gallery waiting for her date to arrive. The windows were tinted quite dark so she was unable to see his paintings from the outside, which she lamented because they were breathtakingly beautiful.

"Claire!" Abe called from across the street. He waved at her and quickly ran across the street.

"Hello, Abe," Claire greeted him with a hug. Abe had presented her with vibrant yellow lilies.

"I have something for you, too," she added.

"A gift? For me? You shouldn't have," he said taking the box. He looked inside and removed a miniature blueberry Danish from it.

"Delicious, as always," he said as he bit into it. He took out another one and placed it in her hand.

"Sharing is caring," she said smiling. Abe laughed at her cute remark.

"I wanted to give you a miniature of something, you know, since you give me miniature paintings. Also, I'm running out of wall space, Abe!" she laughed.

"Thank you for this lovely gesture," he said gently shaking the box. "Where do we start?" he asked. They walked along the streets and admired all of the colorful homes and delightful storefronts. Claire suggested a couple of her favorite restaurants for their lunch later that day since he told her how curious he was about French cuisine. They passed by Claire's old high school and they shared hilarious stories about their high school experience. When lunchtime came around, they decided to rent a canoe and eat while traveling in the canals around the city.

"I'm so glad we did this," Claire told Abe, "It's been awhile since I've had fun." She stuck her hand out of the canoe and dragged it across the water. It was a beautiful, sunny day and the flowers that lined the canals were reflected in the water, making the water appear colorful.

"Thank you for showing me around. Colmar is a truly beautiful city—very charming."

"Do you plan on staying in Colmar?" Claire asked him.

"Should I plan on staying?" Abe asked. He looked at her intently and she knew he was being serious.

"I'm not sure what to say," Claire said looking away.

"I'd love to stay indefinitely if you accompany me on more outings like these."

"Abe, before this turns into anything, I have to tell you something." He nodded his head for her to continue. Claire went on to tell him about her life in America, her infertility leading to her divorce and about how she lost her job.

"I always told myself that if I ever met another man, I would tell him about my inability to bear children so he could decide whether he wants to stay with me or not," Claire finally said. Abe looked out at the water and remained quiet for a long time. Claire thought that maybe he was waiting for the canoe to reach the dock so he could just walk off and forget all about her. Tears filled her eyes but she pretended to look in another direction so he would not see her crying.

Abe cupped her chin with his hand and turned her face to his. He looked into her eyes and said, "I'm sorry to say, Claire, but your ex-husband is a fool." Claire wrinkled her forehead in confusion.

"The ability or inability to make babies does not and should not determine whether a person is loveable or not. It doesn't make a person worth more than the other of being with. You are not disposable, Claire. You are kindhearted and smart and funny and that man was lucky to have you. He's missed out big time," Abe told her. Claire was shocked by his reaction. She thought he'd react the same way her ex-husband had reacted—just completely devalue her as a person. *Why am I so surprised? Of course, he's not like my ex-husband. He's different.* Claire almost caused the canoe to tip over when she leaned in to wrap her arms around his neck.

"Thank you for your kind words, Abe," she said into his ear. Tears of joy still ran down her face. Abe pulled away and wiped the tears with the back of his hand. Claire felt the world around them become silent and blurry; only the two existed on that canal at that very moment. Abe leaned in and kissed her on the lips. The seconds that passed while their lips were locked felt like a frozen moment in time. Claire felt a connection she had never felt before, not even with her ex-husband. With that kiss, she gained a sense of belonging, and she knew right then that she was where and with she was supposed to be.

In the months that came, Claire's mother regained her ability to speak and was slowly regaining her body's mobility but was still unable to help at the bakery. Claire and her father took turns between caring for her mother and running the bakery. The bakery itself, was renovated and Abe's painting of the bakery's exterior hung in the entrance. Abe's card paintings were still on the wall behind the counter. Eventually, Claire was able to earn her teaching credentials in France and became a teacher at Alice's high school. Claire and Abe were married shortly after and ecstatic about adopting their first child. Sometimes, Claire thought about the night that she sobbed in her car at the burger place parking lot and thanked the universe for that rough time in her life—she would not have had the same deep appreciation she had for the new changes in her life.

THE AMISH DEPARTURE

The train screeched to a halt and Elaine Sheldon had to brace herself for the onslaught of people trying to squeeze past out. Holding tightly around the handrail, she winced when a rushing man bumped his laptop bag against her hips, and she took a few steps back with the impact.

The man did not stop to apologize and Elaine only heaved a sigh and fixed her stance as the train resumed moving.

It was supposed to be a five-minute walk from the station to her apartment, but tonight, it did not feel like it. Her steps were slow and her shoulders were drooped. The streetlights refused to turn on properly and it flickered repeatedly as she passed by. Elaine sighed at the dreary atmosphere.

Just a week ago, these walks home passed by with a spring in her step, looking forward to the person who was waiting for her to be back, the person she had been going home to for the past six months, the man who welcomed her with a warm hug and a big smile after a tiring day at work—until the other day.

Her eyes felt heavy and the long wait for the elevator was not helping with her mood. She watched as the red arrow went down as minutes passed by until it reached the ground floor. Her ride back up was spent alone. She smiled bitterly. The world must really hate her.

All doors were closed when she alighted at the twelfth floor except for one. For a second, she almost panicked thinking that the opened door was hers, only to realize that it was the empty unit beside hers. Boxes are stacked in front of the door and the sound of a man's groans can be heard as she came closer.

She battled with herself if she should help or not. As the next-door neighbor, she knew she should, as a sign of welcome for the new occupant, but she also knew that the feeling in her chest is heavier than those boxes. She scoffed at her dramatics but looked down at herself.

Her arms were already crying in protest with her handbag and laptop bag and those boxes looked nowhere near light so she forgot being thoughtful for once and unlocked her door. She was about to go inside when a man's voice startled her.

"Hi. Do you live next door?" The man beamed at her but the smile didn't reach his eyes.

Elaine smiled back, a closed-lip one. "And you must be my new neighbor," she offered her hand which the man accepted. "Elaine."

"Ivan. It's nice to meet you," he let go of her hand and gestured at the boxes. "I'll be done in a minute. You don't have to worry about the noises." He smiled again but Elaine can only see a grimace.

"Don't worry, take your time. I would have helped you but—"

Ivan waved his hand no. "No need. You must be tired from work," he observed, noticing the formal attire and the laptop bag hanging on her shoulders. "Go on ahead. Have a good night."

"You too," she returned in a clip tone and sent a brief smile again before going inside. The bang of the door echoed throughout the dark empty unit, reminding Elaine that she had no company anymore, that she had to spend the night alone in her empty apartment.

A tear escaped down her cheeks, which ended with bouts of sobbing for the third consecutive night.

—-

There are things in life that once you get a taste of, you'd never want to let go. And for Elaine, that was her relationship with Christian.

They started dating a little over a year ago, when they met at a mutual friend's party, though neither are close enough to the celebrant and her friends so they ended up chatting the night away. A week later, they found themselves agreeing to date exclusively.

Elaine did not have high hopes with her relationship at the start. Christian seemed to be the happy-go-lucky type of guy who always acted on a whim instead of having plans. She wasn't in too deep yet, so she didn't mind it at all.

But as the months go by and their relationship turned for the better, people around them started to notice—that Christian is changing for the good and it was mainly because of his relationship with Elaine. It flattered the female, she won't deny it. Knowing that she may be one of the reasons why Christian was trying to find a stable job, having the courage to pursue his passion in photography, and planning for his future, made her pleased.

All along, Elaine was expecting that she was included in the plan. It only dawned on her that she was never part of the picture when one day, she got home, expecting the smell of pepperoni and cheese for their usual pizza night, only to find a large bag filled with all of Christian's things that had accumulated in her home. They never agreed to stay together officially but they might as well be for all the days and weekends the male had stayed with her.

At first, she thought he was going for a vacation. She could've accepted it, a six-month out of the country trips to take images of the wonders of nature. What she didn't understand was why he had to break up with her.

They could've made it worked, Elaine believed so. She trusted herself to stay faithful and she put the same amount of trust on Christian. It just so happened that her ex-boyfriend did not believe in long distance relationships. It even hurt more when he said that he's not even sure if he's even coming back. His career was just starting, he said. It could be his one in a lifetime opportunity, he said. All Elaine could do was cry and beg him to at least try, but he was already decided.

And that was it. The end of a year-long relationship in just a snap.

—

The pastor was going through the sermon part and Elaine pinched her forearm to stay focused. They had to work overtime last night and she barely had a wink of sleep before she raced to be on time to the church.

Attending the mass was a weekly thing for Elaine. Christian never accompanied her no matter how much she forced him to and now, she's secretly grateful because at the least, she has this one activity she was used to doing alone.

The pastor's voice resounded against the walls and she snapped back into attention. Someone, a man perhaps judging by the black slacks and the scent, sat beside her. She almost rolled her eyes for the man's tardiness but bit her lips when she realized that she was no better for drifting off instead of listening.

The pastor droned on and she could hear the sound of the piano and the jingle of the tambourine but it faded as her lids became heavier.

By the time she woke up, people were standing up and were walking towards the exit. Elaine jolted in her seat, lifting her head from a sturdy shoulder she was leaning on, cheeks crimsoning due to the embarrassment.

She looked to her right and her eyes widened while the color of her cheeks got redder. "Ivan," she muttered. Of all people to fall asleep on while a mass was ongoing, it had to be her new next-door neighbor.

Ivan chuckled and raised his hand to his lip, which confused Elaine. When it dawned on her, she turned around and wiped the bit of drool that escaped her lips.

Clearing her throat and checking discreetly if there was still drool left, she turned back again to an amused Ivan. At least now, the smile reached his eyes unlike the first time she saw him.

"I'm sorry for falling asleep on you," she pursed her lips. An old lady passing by gave her a stink eye and she refused to shrink on her seat in shame.

Her neighbor saw the gesture and he chuckled. "It's okay. You went home late didn't you?"

"How did you know?" Her eyebrows furrow.

Ivan looked more amused now. "I heard your door. It wasn't exactly hard to when it's the dead hour of the morning," he explained.

Elaine nodded, laughing at herself for thinking of anomalous things such as Ivan being a stalker or a creep. It crossed her mind that it was still strange for him to be awake at such an hour but then that would mean it was also strange for her to have just come home so she didn't bring it up.

"Oh!" She unconsciously glanced over his shoulder and found a tiny, wet mark. Scrambling for tissues, she pulled a handful and wiped at his clothes furiously. "I am so sorry," she apologized repeatedly until Ivan had to hold her hand to stop her.

"It's spit. No big deal. No one's gonna die," he smiled once again. Elaine thought he should smile more often. It brightens up his face. Meanwhile, her face was on fire.

"Can I treat you for coffee then? As sorry and welcome?"

"I'd love to but I have somewhere to be. Maybe next time," he said noncommittally.

"Next time then." She apologized again before racing back home. A loud 'I'm home' is on the tip of her tongue but she stopped herself just in time.

Elaine dragged her feet to the sofa and flopped down unceremoniously with her legs hanging on an arm. Tears cascaded down her temples, which progressed into sobs. Her chest felt tight and her breath was constricted.

Earlier, she prayed to God to give her Christian back. She wished that Christian would change his mind and call her, or at least send her a message, saying sorry and that he wants her back.

She was praying but the pain hurt like hell. She asked God why did this have to happen to her, why she had to feel such pain, why she had to feel hopeful for her future for once, only for it to crumble right in front of her.

It was so unfair. She gave it her all but all she got was nothing.

—-

It had been a month since the breakup and Elaine was faring better. She haven't cried herself to sleep for two weeks now and she even had the energy to go out for a walk. It wasn't much but it was a start. She still thought of her ex-boyfriend from time to time, which was inevitable considering every corner of her apartment reminded her of him, but the pangs were getting less painful. In a way she didn't know how, she was getting by.

It was a Sunday and she was on her way to the church. A friend, Leslie, welcomed her with a hug.

"You're looking great, dear." The shorter female brushed her cheek against Elaine's and Elaine had to chuckle at her affections.

"Hi, how have you been? I haven't seen you here lately?"

Leslie beamed at her in delight. "I went on a vacation with Luis to France. Oh, we have to get some coffee later. I have lots of stories to tell you," she narrated giddily, the smile never wavering off her face.

"How's Christian? Still sleeping I bet?" Leslie chuckled and Elaine's eyes twitched. She swallowed a lump in her throat and an awkward silence passed before her friend realized that something was wrong.

"Hey, what's wrong?"

Elaine cleared her throat and forced a smile. "W-we broke up," she cursed at herself for stuttering. It felt more real every time she had to say it outloud and it doubled the sharp pain that coursed through her.

Leslie looked shocked beyond belief at the news and scrambled to wrap her arms around Elaine again. "I'm so sorry!"

Elaine, who had to fight the tears that were threatening to come out, hugged her back, glad to have someone to comfort her even if it was a month late. "It's okay. It's been a month."

She pulled back and wiped the tears that escaped despite her resistance. "I'm all right," she forced out a smile. Her friend looked at her worriedly but let it go for now. "All right, let's have lunch together okay?" Leslie asked, to which Elaine said yes. It had been a while since she had a meal with another person aside from her co-workers and she welcomed the thought now more than ever.

The mass lasted for a little over an hour and Leslie pulled her to a nearby Italian cafe that served great pasta and gelato. Elaine was grateful for the distraction but she could not help but glance at a table for two at a corner. She mentally sighed and erased the memories in her head.

—-

Elaine was working on a report when a call came. Not expecting anybody, she looked at her phone quizzically, which registered Leslie's name. Leslie rarely contacted her through the phone.

Surprised, she accepted the call and had to brace herself for a joyful Leslie who almost screeched a 'hello.'

"Hey, what's up?" Elaine reclined back on her seat and shut her eyes. She could hear her stomach grumbling only to remember that she didn't eat anything for lunch.

"I know this might be too soon, but it's been two months and it's not too soon right?" She said rapidly and Elaine had to sit up straight again and focus on her words to keep up.

"What exactly might be too soon?"

Leslie paused dramatically. Elaine could almost hear her excitement through the receiver.

"Dating."

"Dating?" Elaine repeated dumbly.

"Yeah, dating. I figure it's about time you meet new people. What do you think?" Elaine processed everything before saying an alarmed 'what' as a reaction.

She sighed before continuing. "Leslie, I know you have the best intentions in mind. But if you still didn't know, I barely have time to meet new people."

"But you have the time," Leslie insisted. "Every Sundays. Don't you always save your Sundays?"

"I do. But that's for church and some me time. I don't feel like going to a party or anything after a mass."

"Exactly. For church. And forget the me time, you have more than enough of that," Leslie paused and apologized for the insensitive remark, which Elaine only waved away. Leslie was just telling the truth.

"What I actually wanted to say is that I know this guy, from the church we go to, who you might be interested to meet," Leslie drawled on. It took a minute before it registered what she was suggesting.

"Are you setting me up on a blind date?" She asked incredulously.

"Uh, yes," her friend admitted sheepishly.

Elaine rubbed a thumb on a temple. "Do I have a say on this?"

"Not really. I already set up the time and date."

"Leslie—!"

"I had to! I know you're gonna say no!"

"Whatever. Just text me the details. I have work to do," Elaine grumbled. She heard a faint 'I love you' before she hung up the phone and she felt a little bad for not saying it back to her dear friend.

—-

That night, Elaine turned and tossed on her bed. She couldn't stop thinking about the blind date and she had bombarded herself with too much questions that only left her more confused and doubtful.

Is it too soon? What if Christian knows about it? What if the guy isn't what she's expecting him to be? But then, what exactly are her expectations?

The fact that he goes to her church is a good point, but the thought that she saw it as a good point gnaws at her guilt. It might be ridiculous but she felt guilty for indirectly saying yes to the blind date. It had been two months but thinking of a possibility of a relationship with anyone other than Christian brought a bad taste to her mouth.

—-

Elaine pushed the glass door open before a waitress assisted her to her seat. A man was already seated at the table, but she could not see his face yet.

A gasp escaped her lips when the waitress stopped and gestured at their table, making the man look up.

"Elaine?" Ivan said, sounding shell-shocked himself.

"You're Leslie's friend?" Elaine asked for good measure. She had not seen her neighbor for weeks now. The last time, they only exchanged brief hellos when they happened to meet while taking out trash.

Ivan stood up and helped her pull her seat back, before returning to his own side.

"And you are Leslie's friend," Ivan jokingly deadpanned. Elaine took her seat and began to chuckle. Ivan, amused by the situation, also began to laugh.

"I guess we'll be having a date today?" He asked with a smile on his face. Elaine hummed in affirmation while smiling from ear to ear.

"How did you meet Leslie?" Elaine asked once their food was served.

"I actually knew Luis first. He was an old friend and he was the one who suggested this place for me to move to," Ivan explained before taking a bite of the grilled chicken.

Elaine took a sip of water before responding. "Why did you move? Was it for your job?"

The question froze Ivan for a second before he relaxed. Elaine bit her tongue for the question which obviously hit a nerve.

"You don't have to answer it if you don't want to," She said softly.

"Sorry," he offered a timid smile.

"It's okay," she smiled before diverting the conversation to a different topic.

It turned out that they have a lot of similar interests than they could have expected. They have the same fascination with the Harry Potter series, the same geeky side when it came to Star Wars, and the same passion when it came to football—though Elaine loved Man U with a passion while Ivan preferred Chelsea.

Hours later, they found themselves laughing comfortably around each other while they walk together home. They stopped when they reached Elaine's door and Ivan kept a good distance, to which Elaine was grateful for.

"I really had a lot of fun," Ivan smiled.

"Me too. I think it's been ages since I've laughed that much," Elaine gushed.

He put his hands in his pant's back pockets and Elaine mentally chuckled.

"We should do this again some other time?" It was more of a question rather than a statement.

Elaine let out a deep breath she didn't know she had been holding and nodded. "Sure."

—-

She threw the frame inside the black plastic bag and flinched at the sound of breaking glass. Next were the t-shirts and boxers that were definitely not hers, followed by other toilet utilities that were never meant for a woman.

It was a day after her blind date and last night, she had the urge to throw away everything that reminded her of Christian. It had been months but she still kept some of his belongings that he left there, silently holding on to the hope that he would come back.

This move did not mean anything but a sign of her trying to move on. She had been meaning to do it for weeks but the date with Ivan was the last push she needed to start working on it. She sniffed and sobbed for the first few minutes but it got better as the plastic bag got fuller.

It was filled with pictures, letters, dried flowers, candy and chocolate wrappers, and almost every single thing that Christian gave her during their relationship, including the bracelet that he gifted to her last Christmas. It took a lot of emotional effort but afterwards, she felt lighter, as if an invisible baggage was thrown away.

The door next to her opened just as she was pulling the plastic bag outside to throw it in the bin. Ivan looked as surprised as she was. He was sporting a shirt paired with loose shorts and running shoes.

"Going for a run at night?" She asked, eyeing his outfit.

Ivan shrugged. "The park's good enough for some laps."

Elaine stopped for a second to think before taking a leap of faith. "Mind if I join you?"

—

The night was a bit chilly but fortunately, there was minimal wind.

Elaine had been living in that neighborhood for years but it was the first time that she jogged at the park. She always thought it was full of rowdy teenagers getting drunk or creeps who had nothing better to do with their lives. Ivan laughed at her when she voiced it out.

"This place's actually good," He panted, arms swinging as they jogged around the vicinity. "You should just avoid Friday nights because it can be too crowded."

She looked at him curiously. "How long have you been going here?" She asked, breaths coming short. Ivan slowed his pace a bit.

"Since the first week I moved," he answers. "It was a bit lonely staying indoors."

Elaine stopped in her tracks, causing Ivan to stop too.

"I am so sorry for being a very unwelcoming neighbor. I should have made you something and came over to check on you."

Ivan rested a hand on her head and ruffled her hair. Elaine felt like pulling away but didn't, surprised at how large his hand felt. "No need to feel sorry. I know it wasn't your best day then," he continued jogging and she followed automatically.

She gulped as she remembered that day. It was definitely one of her most miserable days. "Yeah. My boyfriend just broke up with me a few days before that," she chuckled dryly. This time, it was Ivan who stopped first.

"I am so sorry to hear that."

She pursed her lips in thought. "It's okay. I've been doing great. It wasn't an excuse to not welcome you," she patted his shoulder, signaling him to continue moving.

It was silent for a few minutes before Ivan spoke up again.

"I just got divorced a few months ago."

Elaine screeched to a halt. "What?" Her eyes widen at her rude reaction. "I mean, when?"

"A few weeks before I moved," Ivan looked down. "My ex-wife and I just got divorced and I realized I can't stay at our home for long so I sold it, and moved here," he gestured at his surroundings with feigned enthusiasm. "And I think I made a great decision."

Elaine took a step closer before wrapping her arms around him. "I am sorry to hear that."

She could feel him shaking his head as he hugged her back. "I guess we're both sorry to hear about each other's heartbreaks?" he joked to lighten the mood. She pushed him back and hit him lightly on the chest before laughing.

They both broke into fits of laughter, earning the questioning looks of the passers-by.

—

They continued to contact each other throughout the week. They may be neighbors but Elaine frequently opted to work until late night so they can't really meet much. Leslie called once to check on how the date went and squealed when Elaine responded with a simple 'Thank you' and shouted 'I knew it, I knew it' repeatedly until it burned Elaine's ears.

The following Sunday, Elaine and Ivan agreed to go to the church together, causing Leslie to get excited upon seeing them.

She looked at them knowingly and winked at Elaine, who blushed at her friend's action. Ivan chuckled at the sight but pretended that he did not see it. All of them, including Luis, Leslie's boyfriend, sat side-by-side inside the church.

During the mass, Elaine prayed and asked for guidance, if what she was doing was right or if it was too soon to consider liking a different man. When she opened her eyes and looked at Ivan's direction, she found him to be staring back at her.

She glanced away and fought down the blush that crept on her cheeks.

—

It was a Wednesday night and usually, Elaine would still be at work, doing things that were not really urgent.

When she got home, it was way too early for bedtime and she found herself thinking of the man living in the unit beside hers. Curiously, she laid an ear flat on the surface of the wall to check for any noises. She didn't know why but she wanted to check if Ivan was home.

She could hear a faint sound of music and she thought about it once, twice, and multiple times before deciding to send him a message.

A few minutes later, there were knocks on her door. Elaine, already clad in more comfortable clothes, welcomed the sight of Ivan carrying chips and soda.

"Did you bring any DVDs?" She helped him bring the things to her living room and settled them on the coffee table. Ivan reached for his back and pulled out some cases and handed them to her.

She raised her eyebrows at the choices. "So you're basically suggesting we watch the whole series of Harry Potter?" She looked at him pointedly.

Ivan shrugged before making himself comfortable on the couch. "Pretty much," he grinned.

In the middle of the movie, they found themselves sitting close to each other, shoulders almost bumping. Elaine looked at her side and it was only a few inches away from Ivan's. Unconsciously, she continued to stare until he looked back.

"Like what you see?" he grinned mischievously, earning a smack on his chest.

"Your scar," she started, pertaining to a small scar at the left corner of his lips.

"Ah, they're battle scars," he jested. Her forehead scrunched at the vague answer.

Ivan sighed before reclining fully. "I had a bit of a scuffle last year. I saw my then wife with another man and I confronted them right on the spot. And the rest is history," he smiled but the bitterness was pronounced.

Elaine copied his position and leaned her head on his shoulder. It was a bold move and she was holding her breath if the male would shrug her off. However, Ivan lifted his arm and rested it on her shoulder so she could scoop closer. Elaine let the tension seep out of her body.

"I only have one question," she said after a while.

"What is it?" He closed his eyes, hoping that he could answer it whatever the question was.

"He got it worse right? I mean, you managed to hit his face at least twice? With bruises?"

Ivan burst out laughing. "Yes, yes, I did. I kicked him in the stomach, too. It was pretty satisfying," he answered, still chuckling at the unexpected question.

"Good," She said before placing an arm over his stomach.

They watched the rest of the movies in the same position.

—-

Elaine was typing her report when her boss approached her.

"I read your latest report, about the success rate if the company decides to venture in e-commerce." She waited with bated breath. It was a report she had been working extra hard for.

"And I can say I'm impressed. I sent a copy to the higher-ups and we just have to wait for their comments," he patted her on the shoulder.

Elaine beamed and said thank you.

"You should continue doing what you've been doing recently," he commented, puzzling Elaine.

"I mean, you look happier. Whatever the reason is, continue doing it," he said before turning back to his office.

Elaine could only think of one big change in her life recently. Biting her lips to stop herself from grinning too widely, she smiled at the thought of a man.

—

She was preparing the TV and the player for their usual movie night when Ivan received a call. His expression dimmed and his jaw locked when he saw who was calling but still answered it, walking towards the kitchen for some privacy.

Elaine, though worried, stayed where she was and fiddled with her own phone. She tried to give Ivan the privacy he needed but was surprised when his voice got louder.

"I don't give a fuck about it. I'm deleting your number. Please don't call me anymore."

She could hear the sound of a phone hitting the floor and she scrambled off the sofa to check on him.

Ivan was staring at the broken device and his chest was heaving deeply. Slowly, she walked towards him and reached for his shoulders. He relaxed at the touch and rubbed a hand on his face.

"I'm sorry you have to hear that," he reached for her hand and pulled her closer to him before hugging her waist.

Elaine put her hand on his hair and carded her fingers through the black strands.

"It was my ex-wife," he explained, making Elaine halt her actions for a moment. She only resumed when Ivan nudged her hand with his head. "She was telling me about her wedding in two weeks, and that I'm invited." He laughed bitterly. "She cheated on me and she had the guts to invite me to her wedding."

Elaine, now shaken, fought the tears that are threatening to spill. She can feel the hurt from Ivan's voice and it was affecting her more than it should.

She remained silent, listening to Ivan's breath until he completely relaxed and his breaths evened out.

The silence was deafening until Elaine had the courage to break it. "Do you still love her?"

It was a yes-no question but Ivan didn't respond for the next two seconds, nor even for the next minutes.

Feeling defeated, Elaine pulled herself from his grasp, ignoring his pleas to make her stay. She collected her things from his living room before walking her way outside and into her own unit. Ivan knocked on her door for a few minutes until she said from the other side.

"Please. Stop it. I need some time alone."

The knocks stopped, and a few seconds later, another door was shut.

—-

Just months ago, it was Christian who was the cause of Elaine's sleepless nights. It was him who was the reason why she cried and continuously asked herself of what's wrong with her and why do people find it so hard to love her. It was him who was the reason why she didn't want to wake up to face another day and tempted her to just laze on her bed, feeling as if all the energy had been sucked out from her.

But now, just a few months later, Ivan had been occupying her mind much more than she expected he would.

He is a good man. He's nice, funny, responsible, smart, and even good-looking—a complete catch if she dared say. When she first saw him, all sweaty and panting from carrying heavy boxes, she just saw him as just another attractive man who happened to be her neighbor and nothing else. Admittedly, she even forgot about him until their embarrassing encounter at the church. That was how it was, but because of one date, it turned into something more.

Elaine found herself genuinely enjoying Ivan's company as they spent more time together. It started from scheduled dates and movie nights until they found themselves into a routine of being together every other day, whether it was to just talk, share about their day, or watch movies.

It was a routine that they easily adapted too—they never forced themselves into it nor did they set fixed days and to-do lists whenever they meet. Day by day, Elaine found herself thinking of her ex-boyfriend less, and whenever she did, it was to smile at the memories they shared and never to wallow in the sadness and the gaping hole he made when he left.

As Ivan made her feel light-hearted, carefree and secured, she found herself forgetting about the heartbreaking nights, about the times when she went back to an empty home, and about the thrown away pictures and gifts. With Ivan, she felt that she could try again, that she could, maybe, fall in love again.

But it seemed that Ivan thought otherwise. She could still see how hurt he was when he talked about his ex-wife inviting him to her wedding. She could remember how tightly clenched his fists were and how much he was trembling in anger. It was a sight she never expected to see from the usually composed man.

When she asked that question she wasn't hoping for an absolute no. They were married and she knew that he must have felt so strongly for her to ask for her hand. But at the least, she was expecting something along the lines of 'I'm doing fine' or 'I'm getting over it' and it would have sufficed, for her at least.

If anything, it made her realize how much she was wearing her heart on her sleeve yet again. She wasn't in love with him, not yet at least, but she knew she was on her way. All along, she thought he felt the same, that he was moving forward and trying to forget his past heartbreak, just like her. Elaine thought that a part of him had thought about her in a romantic way, that she might be someone who he can ideally like, but then again, those were just Elaine's assumptions.

The problem with her, as always, were her hopes and baseless assumptions. These always manage to fuck her emotionally—big time. She just never learned.

—

Ivan tried to contact her in the following days but she was resolved on avoiding him for a few days. She was aware that she was being immature but she deemed herself unprepared.

Every day, she recited every line she could say once they managed to talk. She imagined different scenarios and how she would react to them and what she should say. She admitted, most of her though-of situations were bad. She wasn't too hopeful that they would be returning back to the friendly yet flirty camaraderie they had formed.

Elaine was far from being level-headed. When it came to feelings, she was like an open book. She never tried to hide what she was feeling nor did she ever lie about it. So when one day, while standing on the train, hand clasped tightly on the handrail, and a man stood behind her and asked "Will you be my girlfriend?" she broke down in tears and attracted the attention of other commuters.

Among all the scenarios she imagined in her head, this wasn't how it was supposed to be. He wasn't supposed to show out of nowhere and tell her things she has been wishing to hear for weeks in the middle of a crowded train. She tried to stop her tears but the various emotions overwhelmed her.

Ivan had panicked, wiping away her tears furiously with his fingers and then the sleeves of his sweater. He was expecting her to shriek or push him away or to give him the finger, but this wasn't in his imagined reactions.

When the train stopped at the next station, he gently guided Elaine out and continued hushing her. Her cries were now reduced to sobs and Ivan cursed at himself for making her cry.

Once she was calm, she smacked him hardly on his chest, before saying a garbled "Yes."

For a while, Ivan was confused why she said that but broke into a large grin when he realized the implication.

Overjoyed, he grabbed her face with both hands and kissed her, right in the middle of the station, with some bystanders looking away from the scene. The kiss was chaste yet sweet. Their lips glided smoothly against each other and for a while, Ivan was tempted to press harder, which was futile when Elaine pushed him.

"But," Elaine sniffed and shushed him with a finger on his lips. "Explain."

"Could I take you home first? It's starting to get cold," he gestured at her working clothes—a thin blouse and a pencil skirt—and led them outside and hailed a cab.

There was a deafening silence throughout the ride home and their way up in the elevator, but Ivan never let go of her hand the whole time.

He led them to his unit instead of Elaine's and she was about to protest but he insisted.

He pushed her until she was seated on the sofa and he sat beside her as closely as possible. She squirmed in her seat and he gave her some space, rubbing his neck sheepishly.

He reached for her hand and turned his body towards her.

He started with a deep breath before launching to his long narrative. "That night, when you asked me if I still loved her, I was sure that my answer was no," He brought a hand up when he saw that she was about to interrupt him.

He continued once she silently agrees to keep on listening.

"But at the same time, I can't say it. It sounds more real once you say it out loud doesn't it? Am I making any sense?" He chuckled. Meanwhile, Elaine responded that yes, she understands because she felt the same thing with Christian.

"We were a couple since high school, and then through college. Most people called us the ideal couple and were just waiting for us to get married. It was as if there was no other way out of it but to build our own family. So I did ask for her hand in marriage and she said yes." Ivan heaved a deep breath, composing his next words in his mind.

"But as soon as we started living together, something felt...weird. A year later, I realized how used we are to being together. We were so used to seeing each other, to doing things together that it only seemed natural that we got married. I realized that maybe, we took marriage for granted, and it was a hurried decision merely out of obligation because of the people's expectations."

"We started to drift away from each other then. In the back of my mind, I knew she was thinking the same thing. When I saw her with another man, it hurt me—not because I still love her but because I was at least expecting that we wouldn't reach that point where we would hide secrets behind each other's backs—especially a lover at that."

"I saw red and then I found myself furious. I was angry at her but more at myself for letting us be trapped in that situation. When we decided on the divorce, it was heartbreaking but it felt like a burden I never knew I had was lifted from me. It felt liberating." He paused, tightening his hold on Elaine's hand. Elaine returned the gesture, egging him to go on.

"I admit. It still hurts. But not because I still love her but more from the fact that I spent so many years thinking I was happy but realized that I wasn't. It was hard coming to terms with that: that I forced myself to think that everything was alright when it wasn't. And then suddenly, she told me the news that she's getting married and practically screaming at me that she's found her happiness. I'm happy for her. We've been together for so long that I can't even bear thinking of hating her. But then I thought of myself and my sorry state of a coward who can't even ask you to be mine and I was enraged because I felt that it was unfair. I thought that I deserve my own happiness too." His voice trembled then and he blinked repeatedly as his eyes began to get misty.

Elaine knelt beside him and pulled his head to her chest, rubbing his back consolingly at the confession.

"I'm sorry if I hurt you. Because all these just came crashing on me and I suddenly couldn't answer. I didn't know where to start. It felt too much." She felt a wetness on her arm and hugged him more tightly. If she could only take a part of the pain he was feeling, she would do it.

"I'm sorry for assuming the worst, and for not giving you a chance to explain." She muttered, kissing a spot in his head to reassure him that she was there, and she won't be leaving anytime soon.

Ivan retreated and pulled her into his lap, resting his forehead against hers. "I'm sorry for giving you the chance to assume the worst, then. If anything, I just really want to say how much I like you and how much you make me happy." He gave her a peck and kept his lips there, feeling the smile forming on his lips.

"I'm really glad I met you. I'd do anything I could so you could forget him completely."

Elaine shook her head no in protest. "No, Ivan. We will work together so we could heal completely. This is no you helping me, nor me helping you. This is us helping each other," she said, gazing into his eyes lovingly.

He smiled a smile that reached his eyes, the one that Elaine absolutely adored, before replying. "I love the sound of that."

END